ZENITH IN THE WILL OF LOVE:

The Extreme Situation of Winckelmann,

A Novel in Serial Poems 

ZENITH IN THE WILL OF LOVE:

The Extreme Situation of Winckelmann,

A Novel in Serial Poems | Scott Worth

ABOUT THE CONTENTS

A set of sublime poems collected in a book that tells a story of powerful interest, Scott Worth's Zenith in the Will of Love is bound to reward the reader who efforts to enter the intricate world of his tone-setting, scene-staging, point-making icons. As this series of epitome poems outsets his deft retelling of a life based on the historic figure of art historian Johann Winckelmann of Germany and Italy, he mixes swift or pausing narration with droll or serious observation to grow a mood that impels encounter in a sort of slow rush to the illuminating end in this book that sheds light for mind as well as sense. Winckelmann lived in cling of idealism from peak to peak in some of the earth's most dramatic places each of them backdrop to some of the world's most sumptuous domiciles, entering which Zenith's thread moves in a decorous race to show how a man born poor grew to be a powerful force on minds of the richest men of his times. Outsider due to inner nature, the impoverishment he experienced put Winckelmann's life forward out of need though use of him interwove the worlds of ancient art and modern code in order to make perception new while make social change possible. In bringing life to antiquities through the written word, he redrew the norms of men right in the enclave of his most repressed contemporaries up to the point he created the same a hotbed for the revival of ancient consciousness in men. As a final touch to seal his effect Winckelmann was murdered the fact of which Scott Worth uses for a continuous subtext to create a feeling of suspense in eclectic material which in turns eddies to disclose combinations of hidden truths or sallies to reveal implications of open lies. To equate each page with a portrait or a perspective else a scene or a time period, Zenith's procession of serial poems captivates to draw in the reader each page for a stimulus fix, so letting intrinsic of suspense coincide with that of the developing plot, to cause the reader's unworded wonder how will the strict bounds of the poems continue to fulfill the ever-more-elaborate demands of the deepening story. In the end it is just the reading experience itself that discloses how the plot is embodied poem to poem for the impressive reveal of its development. In the meantime Zenith dispenses qualities of the novel in a slew of settings, situations, and characters some of which include the court of Nöthnitz, the court of Potsdam, the Vatican, the port of Trieste, the crossing of the Alps, the reception of Lord Baltimore, the reception of a pope, the climbing of Vesuvius, the swish but virtue-bound Count von Bünau, the cunning but compassionate Cardinal Archinto, the beneficent but double-dealing Cardinal Albani, the cordial but rebellious Baron d'Hancarville. As the life of Winckelmann grows in complication the reader watches him enter a prolonged dance with death introducing the most complicated invention of the roles here in the person of Francesco Arcangeli. Zenith's tone is changed with his first step into its pages while it follows the evolving relations in his join of Winckelmann for a final week's wait. In the time Zenith uses minimalism to reinvent eighteenth-century verse for impact, it tends itself a metaphor of part of the Winckelmann effect in the stress he put on form even on its bid to become a unique epitome in the world of classic models.

QUOTATION

The rules of biography require truth. Do not write anything that is not well founded or that many men know better than to think is. If the Life is to be well written, let the truth appear in it. The goodness of a thing consists in this, that it is what it is and what it should be.

Johann Winckelmann in a letter to Muzel von Stosch

A BRIEF COMMENT ON OUTSETTING

In spite of the optimism of his times embedded in the quote, I opt else in this mood-cloudier novel in serial poems using the imagination this form implies; Zenith in the Will of Love is in part a poet's retelling of the historic life-on-record of Johann Winckelmann though is in part a droll relating of the chronology of a crime he suffered, required of both parts to use the acquiescent equilibrium I intuit is true of us to persuade me that his spirit might tolerate his portrait in this book, this same thing possible to state for soul-unrulier Francesco Arcangeli if just to consider the treatment he received in life; I invent without remorse on Heinrich von Bünau, counting on his spirit to leave his name to needs of the present fiction not meaning to bias perception of his real qualities, this same thing possible to state for the spirits of Alberico Archinto, Alessandro Albani, cook-hiring counts Bardi and Baldinotti, as well as others drawn in romantic or contentious lines of relation including Inspector Schnackenburg who though is presented in a moment of stress ended up writing a letter which Winckelmann used to recommend him for his role in service of the mentioned von Bünau; I trust that the spirits of incidental-to-it individuals whose names I omit will not mind contributing to the story in relative obscurity.

Scott Worth

1

IN COSMIC TIME,
THE TWO MURDER JOINS STILL UNEMBROILED BOYS

Would these let sight connect boy-boy ones outlooked
To selves bound stood in views of beauty-posed cause,
Time would be one composite owed just thought's use,
To eternize two in the best form both took.

So dream be on shore worlds touch off the stood rock,
To show the two connect sight their each choice holds
A beat long in posed weigh of doom these both house,
Each slow to trust or tell if one should show rogue!

One to be caused his earned death sentence took else;
One chose up from his childhood to be so great
His *murder* should re-pounce on poor of bruised selves.

Eternal mist blows off the tossed crests outspread . . . ,
But Schönbrunn stands, order, court just legal dust fills.
On wood strikes the big file Mordakte's brought might.

2

APOLLO
HOLDING TO WINCKELMANN THE IDEAL OF A FORMER TIME OF BEAUTY

How times men tread in moving through tread's eras
Till now with matter ringed we bring lent thinghood!
Ones wares-swept look up to the dome to sink mood
And cause heart sigh for eras which more nourished!

Now does the blueness teach us when in pure selves
Men did with less but loved theirs best in time stood?
How does ideal form raise high cultured men's truth,
Or this bestow taste which for depth of theirs helps?

The bilge, the dross, the things, the growth diminish
Ourselves who stop none in the mime holds peers stuck . . .
Ones swept on spread of circuits plumb with endless

Wills the home coin-mint sees for billions-forced look
And storm of items to enswirl our wrenched lives
And throw wept souls on simulation's world mocked!

3

WINCKELMANN,
MAN OF THE HOUR IN TIMES OF THE BLIGHT OF ROCKETING OVERPOPULATION

Tell world who do men seem to be who stand streams
In lure-fond lives owed strength of willing their growth?
The sale grows stirred with things to set our dire truth,
Who more relate to things through too routine mimes.

Too swift we leave the world when just it strengthens
Us with the nature grows who slain feed more growth!
Our looks so seldom see them when some fur's group
On tar looms up trailed in the truck's steel then stands

A quaint fur of its cows though ourselves dwell staged
In car-room, in bright-lit home, or in box-light,–
Shown so unreal that tempting's use most wills watch

Of sold things' great destruction which explodes right!
We seem beasts too in matter's ring sensed too much:
How crush control to free our hearts from love's blight?

4

THE POET
THE CHILD OF LOVE ON WINGS TO WINCKELMANN

O storm-bright heart how turn to find who love mine?
One drowned in binds of crowd relationships brought
To blot the world how mine I *mourn* once with growth
Submits to things find-level things which move them!

I look up off the streets bound stood in growth's time,
To pine though scorned for readership to be wrought,
The readers mine to grow in child-pure depth's truth,
Yes with me grow required the child-heart loves men!

O down with things when Greek in mind this life's self
Waits uncompelled, unmiming, poised to bring light!
You too sought love how know till freed for high drift!

One vowed I use mine use heart moving in that
Willed zone of soul the poem transports to let sweep,
But not till sheer mind swept close overwings it.

5

WINCKELMANN
ON WINGS TO HIM INVOCATION OF IT MATERIALIZES

The bar-code world, bits-lined mail, mixed-up box-light,
Wares' popcorn, theft-proof wrap, in-shipment's record
And life's handwriting powers dimmed, ever-spare part,
How make decisions here where mind finds such blight?

The ducts, duct-tape, coiled wires, insulation rolls plied,
Still nothing like the streets that cross this tarred world,
How find us edified by beauty or art,
Once art such so the art of life could draw sight?

Too long it is since reasoned science won earth's men,
Deprived of beauty though willed to conduct growth,
Yes ease the crowd-in-flow result of served mime!

The rote love binds us in routines know no stop,
To let mere hormones house themselves in world pent:
O Winckelmann, Winckelmann come show us how love!

6

A TOWN IN THE ALTMARK

You sweep how does Apollo sweep who parts clouds,
Or lets them part while view descends to reach town,
A town originating in the Saxon
Eastphalian Balsamgau some of the Altmark's forest.

In the Margraviate of Brandenburg is
The town to recognize the bounds owe etched point,
A map men's powers see drawn this map each-owned
In minds which then without more outer search rest.

How charming this town Stendal being charms more
In lurk below the rooftops to end Prussia's,
A Hanseatic League town Teutons fill in termed lore!

High over this the view descends which draws streets
And turns them entrance path to meet one corner
A cobbler's shop which seats a dwelling-house raised.

7

MARTIN THE COBBLER,
ANNA THE WIFE, GRANDFATHER OPA THE WEAVER, JOHANN THE STUDENT

A child observed his source how he might do things
More men did were his structured interest different,
Such child's source Martin Winckelmann to sit bent
A cobbler though might serve in place a true king's!

A child observed his source how she might do things
More women did were means her stationed life lent,
She Anna Meyer her source in his living
A weaver willed his structured interest shown sense.

Sweet Martin, Anna, cobbler, weaver, these formed
Him what he was through birth but could not hold him
To mind his station more than feel his right earned!

More their world charmed his outlook to resolve him:
So much could be redeemed were he in great turn
To meet the world's requirement while best student.

8

1717 TO 1727:
ALIVE TO FIND A SENSE OF BEING IN THE WORLD

A cobbler's child dwelt treated in home's close heart.
The rareness of the treats enhanced ones proved gift
In prelude speech of wisdom, humor's thought-drift,
Tend-richer insight, word-help for the crossed world.

His stare met troubled own likes who in school heard
How each else-raised peer reconciled to slopped life,
In tenser outcome, mouthing off, each forced-up tiff,
And tics or growls which rose in fights head-lowered.

His stare met the cathedral's crowd the group willed
But hopeless not to be themselves in bound wrecks,
Each different to himself or souls heart-home's dwelt.

Then somewhere Jesus was for men's sins punished,
Their wet life sops to seeps with his the blood spilled,
As praised for friend of who on earth is doomed vies.

9

SHOCKS OF SLIM FORM TO VIEW IN THE ALTMARK,
IN STENDAL TOWNHOMES, FIELD WOODS, SCHOOL-ROOMS, CHURCHES, NIGHT-BEDS

The bloom stepped in Apollo touched some neighbor-
Hood sons in perfect form to house bloomed promise.
The winks of some were in foundation-bloom's flesh
The lean form caused to pop for seeing-pleased stare.

The best foundation-bloom winked not when heavier
But when the bloom was working-bloom slim-honest,
The boy Apollo, Antinous, or Adonis,
In general form more so since worked while self-pure.

It lifts one's spirit when forms rise like shown winged;
The grown-fat or the formed-fat grow to weigh down
One's spirit bound to earth when on sight some sink!

He seemed on toes to notice their forms pleased one,
To feel the soul winged more so be own found length
A beast midst ones foundation-bloom's lean *best* own.

10

A CHILDHOOD IN THE SENSE TO PERCEIVE THAT

One seemed to step in past enough stone structures
To mold for beast sensed privilege which enchanted:
His hope loomed off the present privilege-seen light,
And some great end he pictured with evoked worlds.

Yet closed-up buildings hovered in his looked stares,
The buildings ones denied more entrance when met,
To cause him feel doomed till from pitied stance let
Him form will which opposed their put of such force!

He seemed to be one part of tide whose feet walked
The earth of drier rock condensed from stuff burned
As mood in soul or heart . . . Self, soul, light this took

Up to the sun or star sensed source of moved churn!
A force saw entered buildings rocks if reached broke
The stuff still tide spent to its sides in rounds turned!

11

HE ENTERS THE HOME
OF ISAIAH TAPPERT AGED RECTOR OF THE LATIN SCHOOL IN STENDAL

Use is on thought the caused excuse men each need.
The model Homer first-impressed on schooled mind
Went stride-bound with the Jesus model taught him,
Went deeper once to find him one blind's child guide . . .

The student guide for Homer life repeated,
On seeming outlook in the same head in a new time:
The most industrious school-boy was one brought in,
To be the rector's leader, *reader*, helpmeet,

Amanuensis, and surer self in general.
On walking trips theirs double shared a beast's form,
Although their disjoins made poised rest eventual.

Old Tappert weighed his burden which in mixed turn
Was lifted in pronouncements to owe mind's wealth,
And retrospect for learning's tricks own help earned!

12

THE SCHOLAR IN DEN AND ON ICE

At night mind-studious impulse would consume him.
The rector's study then turned child's world delved in,
And books desired books then plumbed from willing
Old Tappert seemed supplanted-dozed near Johann!

So seemed the scholar's post the perch to boost him,
And cause him be the model schoolmates else went
To imitate if could. He helped ones with his teaching,
And sold instruction to buy books his most dreamed.

The sports of his companions sometimes forced him
To join them though if did he put in pocket
The book to plumb in moments stolen from them . . .

At noon on ice he glided off from those did
More turns and tricks though in his mind's rehearsing
Impressed book Greek or Latin with his look set.

13

1730:
THE CHILD JOHANN IN PLUMB OF THE INFINITE

It took some mentor though if none then took books,
To give the child's mind sense of world formed pliant,
To mean the world was chance-supplied its each sign
And each time to combine parts strange on outlooks!

The world's men might involve no matter what cause
And choose succeed no matter what things different.
Each time's own deem theirs is the mode for triumph
If though remake-life men find change in code books.

The books themselves lure who must note things so bound:
The long-received of them exist in bound sets
The richer than the nearer text still draws one.

The richer-bound texts if to plumb help one reads,
To find sheer possibilities' heights caused one
Once opens up thing infinite brought owned stretch!

14

HOW MARTIN THE SIRE
INSTILLS WISDOM HE IS TO REMEMBER SO IT GUIDE HIM IN HIS STEPS

One poor the father of the sole son helped child,
And child to find he chance relived to see stretch
Who seemed some strained to meet on need the basics,
His heart repeated his sire's cause of willed help.

Such father sought to make secure the child's life,
To counsel learn theology, mathematics,
And medicine as well as read his classics,
So real-world skills joined character-to-build self!

A father how deep this was to his thought-walks,
Once impetus ebbed so caused his drawn mind's growth . . .
A force self seemed if own inertial mood-brooks

Saw pictures in remembrance of times lent both:
In lives served different-timed deaths not to owe books,
His store he put up of how toil-coped ones loved!

15

EDUCATION UP TO HIS ENTRANCE AT HALLE

The wrath housed in the wounded heart of man Greek
As great Akhilleus-housed wrath lured the boy's heart.
To read wide cohorts of them each the cohort,
What number now's poets proud to be read none read

Strong Homer peerless in power poets read none seek!
How could the boy foreknow the climax though stirred
To read the first few pages in their glow swart,
Appearing in them manlier themes owed man piqued?

His time went Köllnisches- to Altstädtisches-schooled,
Berlin to Salzwedel. 1738 saw
Him enter University of Halle soul-

Instructed student of theology ja.
He more pursued his Greek in school of self-rule,–
Books that placed men's essential selves in states raw!

16

HE ENTERS NOW A GRAMMAR SCHOOL IN BERLIN

A wind took whiff of fall round leaf-blown pent fields;
His fall perception went schooled up in strange times
Aseating outskirts of Berlin's school-benched friends,
To own on timeless outlooks Neu-Kölln's seen swells.

In school like in some creche chance interchange lies;
So seems it that two self-perceived could lend sense
To each else while without for seem to change minds,
To cause perception smooth-persist for themselves!

He might be any of his peers though seem to outlook
In unchanged sense once interchanged like-met heads,
And in migration move round so their thoughts broke

On each else though no different look or seem these!
So here he was own-destined sakes whose school took
Him round in peers since grew to feel in mixed selves!

17

1733 TO 1736:
THE SELF OR THE SHELF OF LEARNING'S WEIGHT

Meek zeal for learning more for pleasing marked him:
Old Tappert's love turned Rector Backe's lived shown
Him brought this time to draw change so be lessoned
Some under Tappert's friend lent the boy there sent.

In time held-open lectures on belles-lettres lurked in,
He clinched his growth in the Cologne Gymnasium.
In public lectures he heard of a passed man,
And dead Fabricius' library's dispersion.

He cut the neck's hole out of smooth board six feet,
And this he carried hand-held to the sale in
Fabricius' house in Hamburg though paused with it,

To call on nobles, curates, bailiffs for donation.
His bid for books brought him their weight exquisite:
Yoked under this board he the walking shelf seemed.

18

HE ENTERS NOW A HIGH SCHOOL IN SALZWEDEL

Turns in the world took life round to note fall change.
1736 he went in cool stare
To be enrolled in school of the Gray Cloister,
Went long in chart of school enrollment's self strange.

He took two meals of week perched on a built bench
In home of the town's printer one Herr Schuster.
His board on weekends paid him to be tutor
To this man's step-son Heller sweet his swell length!

The tutor's chance of leisure went to cross toil,
In those hours Schuster seemed required to press on
In meeting print demands closed doors could not halt.

His loitered brow stood over leaflets, read some
Of public bills, but spellbound watched the close skill
Used to set books in rails for printing's pleased mind!

19

AT TWENTY-ONE HE COMES TO TASTE COLLEGE

A stipend brought him college though was too scant
To live on would he not teach too some minds there.
His will complied with patrons willed to enter
Him in the catalogue "theology student".

His great dread of some lonesomeness of such men
Took his soul out of their imposed view's center.
His Hebrew lessons done he would re-enter
His studies of those Greeks which on enthused bent

He prosecuted with piqued predilection.
He translated Herodotus possessed like
Upswept on wings through cherished recreation . . .

To court's town Dresden he went on lone self's trek:
The bailiff Löscher ill-received him in his need when
Aid he could use such rumored patron wished keep!

20

A LIBRARY,
A LECTURE SERIES, AND A SCREAM ON A BRIDGE

His Halle years seemed long since brought extension
To these when he remained with Chancellor Ludwig,
To set his library in order once requested
To take the task his form-pronounced consent won.

Too he brought ear their public speeches when went
To lectures of men Sellius, Hornius, and this Ludwig.
To read how Gaul was conquered saw him quest like
A soldier under Caesar—if brought some strong

Sense of his rash mind in view of neared war's swirl,
On edge of Frankfurt. Turned round rendering back-
Steps on the road he went in self-retreat's hurl,

Till up to one town's bridge mulled his looks' impact.
A scream shot from a coach reached from a rich girl,
To beg who raised his razor *more* weigh being's sake!

21

EDUCATION UP TO HIS ENTRANCE AT JENA

A student who could promise some set output,
He welcomed income but joined other sulkers:
A Lutheran theologian's life seemed not theirs,
And more the mind bug of the called he noted.

A church did wish to fund its own who studied
In medicine when pastors too sought doctors!
In 1740's motive Johann took course-
Work in the town of Jena place he showed drift . . .

A doctor's table rid the general scheme's flesh
He thought to love when not so cool-dissected:
Dissecting his own heart he saw how inwished

Some Athens Socrates in question might stride
And Plato grow beside him in the mind his!
How could he overcome this world to set right?

22

A REGIMENT,
A SLEW OF PUPILS, AND A STUDY OF ENGLISH BESIDE ITALIAN

The high-bred loins, the thick thighs of one's stature,
The heart-won looks, the great poise of the bred life
Imposed the hot form Herr von Grollman's swell self
Held upright in the saddle drew male-swapped stare.

The high-bred hot son too of riding master
Would cause him settle in their swank home himself.
He was the tutor some taught lustier mind's wealth,
While in the Bredow regiment in Oster-

Burg riding men taught him the pleasure looks took.
Applied in Jena from hope medicine's stage
Would stand most interests met in life's betook walk,

He took such number pupils that he strained breaths!
Aid to ones else he toiled sole that in such luck
Learned the Italian learned the nice English language.

23

ATURN
THE CALM TRANSITION JENA TO SEEHAUSEN

At Halle/Jena: His eloquence he won though saw their doctrine
And medicine were not his things who wound up
To step off on his course of self so bound coped,
Deserting campus paths of Halle/Jena, sulked in,

To live with spirit books he might teach tokened.
At Magdeburg: Who *he* was on chance needed will his own truth
In one official's house, dean in one town's drove,
He teacher soon to mentor the broke-books son.

At Seehausen: How long he strove to vie if for a post starched
And shirted just to let him search his watched tread,
To sink except when reading did for soothed quirks!

But 1743 on undisputed
As deputy headmaster he taught proud works
In tongues of romance countries or the Vulgate.

24

THE MOTION OF HIM PUPIL TO PUPIL TO SCHOOL

Would he dispute how friendship brings life treasure?
Town Jena quit he looked to town Berlin fond.
In Heimersleben Lewis von Hans lived on
His freehold sweep in reached space of sweet nature.

The former secretary to the diplomat for
The Danish embassy in Paris now sat wisdom
In quiet retirement though wished his son lessoned,
And Johann's call on him brought double that chore.

Once settled in this friend's home to teach this teen,
He found the invitation from a neighbor
The upper-bailiff Lamprecht to teach his son.

This man would travel to be dean some miles near,
But left his son him who in change of station
Took both his pupils to a school where taught more!

25

PETER LAMPRECHT AS A YOUTH
(ADVANCE ANGEL TO SIRE OF A BROOD AND DULL CIVIL SERVANT)

How was it man should fall in love with teen boy?
He was familiar to boy charm but how was sight formed?
Most men familiar to boy charm would still scorn
Its opted use for feeling such termed-strange joy.

He stood more pliant? Strange heir of a man roi?
Observed things closer? Showed weak in life-lived norm?
Just what formed one more sensitive to fit form?
Ah most lunks never saw that maleness lent joy!

The Lamprecht family's handsome son was Peter . . .
The powerful in norm or wealth no strange thing
Struck to preclude their sharing of room's bed or

Bath what norm in two males find either wanting?
One's friendship welcomed for one's mind to better,
Two minds grew fixed to note the other's ranging.

26

THE ANGELIC SOURCE
OF THE HOMOSEXUAL INSTINCT THE WORLD SUBMITS TO EACH SORDID DEVELOPMENT

Angelic mind springs thought high off pure's body,
Although the same feeds depth from form angelic.
An angel once appears prefigures heights reached
In spirit through the same's impression shows high.

Midst angels, cherubs, or ephebes live those free!
The Lord God's midst dwells angels each of his like,
But on stark earth angelic selves their likes strike,
And these remain to feed in soul-locked looks vie!

The soul transports itself on sweeter form's wings,
And the angelic girl is bettered so lets
The boy find her in boy form, sterile-turned things.

On the angelic boy form mind springs most reach,
And free of natal cause which brings rebirth's chains
Obtains angelic soul's communion-trued heights!

27

THE SCHOOL AT SEEHAUSEN:
DUAL SITUATION OF THE TUTOR AND HIS PUPILS

It was his pupil Peter Lamprecht who would
Be his heart's favorite—though the younger von Hans
Seemed lent relief not to feel those presumed bonds
The pacing rival seemed to feel once caused brought

Sulk midst their lector's deputy-brand room's brood!
The other chose one peer's of common-toned rooms
Two thin beds sailed for walking space scarce unions
To need them form for squeeze except if fond would . . .

Once found decided so behind the shut door,
The deputy gave Peter the one big bed
In theirs his room while took for him the stuffed chair.

At least this chair reclined between books each side,
To let him sleep short nights from twelve till just four.
At six he tutored, eight he lectured, ten to twelve read.

28

HOW IN PLATO'S CONCEPT
THE BEAUTY OF A YOUTH STARTS UP A WAVE OF SPIRITUAL PROGRESS

A process starts that brings the soul transcendence.
The powerful form of a boy's young beauty
Is first to captivate the right soul's stood eye,
So pure transcendence makes on such its entrance!

How does one to detach from first-entranced sense,
When *he* to quit what object rests from what eye
Would ever be its bed just this must not be,
Must leave such on occasion for life's chance means?

Then beauty seems to cling the world the youth lets
His beauty touch in eye of him who finds it
To stand shared with some time-lent others' bodies.

The value is detached still more to cling light
In others' souls whose lovely thoughts promote this,
And then one views the forms transcendent in sight!

29

HOW IN PLATO'S CONCEPT
SUFFERING TO CAUSE WRETCHED DISTRESS LEADS TO AT-ONE-MENT

O it should work in step though something else needs!
The one attracted never would uncling him,
The youth whose beauty makes him feel transcendent,
Without some cause to feel life's void with self's stress.

How progress forms owes suffering world real's reach,
To draw self from the love one should remain in.
One suffers lost love or if not still seems dreamt,
And seldom feels it touch forms else so feels stretched.

One's pain turns one from lust to valuing souls,
Since one seeks light from the first source to shine true
As though to tolerate the wretch one is of dream's loss . . .

One circles to appreciate what seems new,
In empathizing wisdom, well-contained thoughts,
Divine-sourced beauty, endless terms, one sensed flow.

30

SAID IN HIS 1746 LETTER TO PETER LAMPRECHT

The time-real swivel of the stood code caused pained
Detection of self's inner trace when matched Greece!
His followed method worked in models each pleased,
To find just failed his world-since puppet show's time.

His private pupils seemed for Christian loves meant;
But it surprised him that behind their strict selves
He should with more unpeeling find no Greek match,
To match the trace bound to control his own theme!

Each pupil empathized when growth of hope caused
Each overture to grow . . . What happened then drove
Home artless status . . . Deeper love seemed just lost

On its own object's mind shocked feeling *men's* love.
Tender Johann: Ours is a love more than our century's thought loves,
Ours matchless if one code-shaped sends the sin off!

31

EVIDENCE
OF OPINION-FIXED CONDITION-FROZEN LIFE

How Johann Left:　He self-free *praised* warm friendship till the boy froze,
Mind just re-locked in match-life match-will patience.
The love mood's fact-plain doom insulted presence,
And Johann other-roomed not to seem crushed close.

How Peter Left:　Overt life's tone long stood with exile's pause caused
Young Peter's budge till, writing like who self-mends,
It brought return to Seehausen whose reached plans
Saw mind to strengthen on his *master's* put thoughts.

How He Left Twice:　Soon nearness reignited love whose reared form
Of warm expressions startled one's norm-fixed mind:
The boy left Johann's school not to desert norm!

The second time to feel crushed Johann reasoned
That work with children was not his but there turned
Up Friedrich who seemed willing Greece to teach him.

32

FRIEDRICH VON BÜLOW A BRIGHT RELIEF IN TIME

One spin of earth to cause time leaves world riddled,
The mortals spun between moods like of their times.
Most minds hold ever-spun from codes to hormones . . . ,
Worse do power's stands cause souls do inner battle.

His means were strained when in the Prussian Cradle
A summer's poor schoolmaster sought meal-parents
And took paid work to teach in home environs.
He put holes in his clothes fixed with a needle,

Yes strove for independence though lived forced on
The household of some tutored son who showed wiles,
Most his to need watch if would spare his person!

He seldom stoked his fancies not these brought else,
But how neared him one Friedrich who if neared him
Was just pose in moue, motion, mirror-owed depths.

33

HOW HE TIMES IT WITH FRIEDRICH VON BÜLOW

One's love he needed time right would he touch him.
His first love taught him too well how the bliss went,
The bliss that is in times to be said Christian,
As let one slip though to repeat one's shocked mime.

Seehausen's master soon in love with such one,
He loved his moue, his movement, his inmixed mien.
Bound wait-time up to blossom-time lent rich being
The one who sought this to impress on watched him.

Should bid signs pass between them in the sunroom,
The two ran out of house to place just secret
And the one he saw the one he wished owned them!

But this would be disowned once soul would strike it,
To feel restored in code this too seduction
One posed in role which owed norms for its strict set.

34

WINCKELMANN:
MY WHOLE LIFE WILL BE TO RESEARCH THIS LOVE
(SAID IN HIS 1747 LETTER TO FRIEDRICH VON BÜLOW)

The two took Zeus to witness how love bound them,
Two who took selves in joint sweep like in one stride.
The love in them was up from childhood grown tight,
When subject loved love's object each else found in!

Two who were used to looking looked each on them,
And acted on love once empowered with own might.
So risks one bore the other in his wont did,
Wished in the same conditions so were bound blent!

Who were the two men loved . . . ? Pylades! Orestes!
King Agamemnon's son was sent from their home
When Clytemnestra chose to love Aegisthus.

One went home to avenge his father where doomed
To weaken though then Pylades' strength pressed his,
To murder those these did when punished were one!

35

HIS ELUSIVE SUPPORT-DOUBLE:
THE ERASTES IN PURSUIT OF HIS EROMENOS IN THE AGE MOVING UP TO STURM UND DRANG

The love he chose required deep intellect's thought,
And caused that—no point choosing with his senses
The more voluptuous-sensuous role of men's roles—
He take the swash-lent top's part in the sex sought.

One more experienced, one more well-read should
Be reconciled more father figure of the friendship's.
He was the teacher, mentor, when less-seen sleep's
Delights redrew horizons twixt males well-wrought.

Greek love inspired these friendship bounds heroic,
The challenge was to lend thoughts formed on read books
A mind like Friedrich's in the time he showed Greek.

His love-quests based on classic models' lit brooks
Were doomed for how books lore-developed truth like
Won no one time-real code left to feel bred shocks.

36

1747:
A COLLISION WITH INSPECTOR SCHNACKENBURG

A time he lived content; mind was healed in teacher;
Still loomed up over him the ephorus who preached,
A dull Orbilius no true models could teach,
And this Inspector Schnackenburg doomed his peer.

Although Johann could preach if need just be there,
He let this man prepare the preaching most weeks;
Soon tired of Sunday sermons he sought due peace,
And edified himself to be the reader

Of truths not from the Psalm-book but from Homer.
On top of this some friends disclosed his honest
Opinion to the ephorus' dishonor.

A man of mind as light as cork thought-stopped him,
He of bipeds wiper best of Silenus this
Ass the most stupid of the Gods though owed them!

37

COUNT UP:
HE OBTAINS A POST IN CULTURAL SITUATION CLOSE TO HIS OWN HEART

A count was in the world to count on his side.
If sudden seemed sweet rumor how long this took
To reach him was the crime of time up till struck,
More punishment commuted if to write said.

1748. He wrote to Count von Bünau misted.
Johann to Heinrich: Our times put little value on each Greek book
I strive to find then delve in just to feel shock
That this should be true when enriching each read.

More pertinent is that I penetrate them,
Devoted to dig up gems though expensive
And rare each book to wish could easier be mine!

Appointed secretary of the man's deep
Library 40,000 volumes deep near Dresden
At Nöthnitz, Johann went to own his changed life.

38

ASWIRL IN THE READING
HE DID OF ILLUSTRIOUS MEN (COUNT AND WIFE OF HIM SOON TO MEET)

Up out in steps join Nöthnitz stood credentialed
Man Johann whose own reading list was nimbus:
Down out of hat if strip-thin fell the long list
In several slipped scrolls *he* were paper-tinseled!

On one scroll Homer slips opposed in one scroll,
To slip down both sides of his head lent poem-bliss
In couplets Pope formed, ones read since in tongue Greek's.
Herodotus slips down on point eventual

Of Cicero's the Father of History Scribed . . .
Slips down Thucydides the chronicler of Pelop-
Ennesian Wars. Sophocles, Euripides slip.

Slips Xenophon of military history's trove.
Slip Plato, Aristotle. More still then in strips slip,
And swirl till ebb on wind to leave who steps up!

39

AN AMANUENSIS TO COUNT VON BÜNAU

His duty was to help the count in writing
A treatment of the Holy Roman Empire!
He must collect the basis in texts since were
Deserted to owe time's change of men's reading.

In moments off work he could plumb the rich thing
The library was, in timed dance to find here
Voltaire the champion of Enlightenment or
Him Montesquieu philosopher enlightened.

In some books were depicted sculptures lustier.
The nearness of antiquities enticed him:
His budding love of Ancient Greece's sculpture

Side trips to Dresden nourished in excitement.
His interest in art rose from each exposure
To treasures or to artists, place life mixed them.

40

AESTHETICS:
THE APPROPRIATED WORD FOR SENSES SENSIBLE TO STIMULI FINDS INTELLECT

On Alexander Baumgarten's Invention:

The Greeks went to divide cognition thought or
Sensed noētá kai aesthētá their words reached.
Aesthētiká he took reduced to furnish
The word to mean not the five senses but their

One used for varied diet of the embodier.
The sense this was he took to bring to art taste.
A good or bad taste could exist in words' space
To owe connections he developed through tier

Of choice-sets based on pleasure or displeasure.
A deduction of the rules or principles of
Artistic beauty would be reached with measure

Outcome of the Learning in Aesthetics:

Of model individual taste which lifts up.
The theory went from Baumgarten the teacher
To Winckelmann who brings it in so meets love.

41

IMMANUEL KANT
REACTS TO HIS READING OF ALEXANDER BAUMGARTEN'S AESTHETICA

A deduction of its rules or principles on
One individual's taste? On this seized great Kant.
The basis is just observation said saint,
And sensuous-sourced, thing he empirical found.

Taste is the test that is to find these rules sound,
So turn it turns does some critique of taste tend
A name aesthetics better to be left in
The science of sense-findings Grecian halls want.

So either this or let the new aesthetics
Share with the speculative world mused naming,
In part to house its transcendental meaning,

In part to house its value owed noetics.
On Winckelmann's Reading of Them: The founder of art history deemed parse not low,
But Baumgarten long helped who praised Apollo.

42

1749:
ADAM OESER MAKES HIS INTRODUCTION TO HIM

The climbers up in winged domes of great buildings
Included Adam Oeser who bounced down a fit man.
He was a climber through his time spent with grand
Men Gran, Dietrich, Schuppen fixed in willed things.

Up if to look in thought-best rooms sun-filled Wien's
Or Dresden's like the Opera House owed swept span
Is to find off the bouncer-down in each one
Soft-painted skies with people just the height wings.

In Hubertusburg Palace up to throne room,
He did not find home the Elector Frederick
Augustus II though off the high vault bounced down

Was the fit man who touched him with his smile big!
Ich mag dich Mann he said who was to bounce down
In rooms to brush of Nöthnitz brightened with reach.

43

A TRIUMVIRATE'S
UNBID SLIPS OF INFLUENCE TO WIDEN WITH TIME

On long since met him this friend worlds encouraged
Him in pursuit of his aesthetic studies.
One future friend of great Johann von Goethe's,
He Oeser helped two Johanns to be flourished!

So was it Winckelmann went to exert reach
With Oeser's reach to mold him off their brought ties.
The powerful twin influence would grow his
Own influence on Germany for arts each.

The classic showed love's path for painters, sculptors,
And architects this too for scribes and poets.
The torch his drawing teacher taught to hold theirs

Was Johann's held to things Greek things to love best.
Encomiums on rediscovered sculptures
To show his burning heart stirred Europe's new quest!

44

THE NUNCIO
TO THE SAXONY COURT AT DRESDEN ARCHINTO

How come men search for friends or lovers of them?
One owes to these their bearing on one's whole life!
Acquaintance might change private course or truth if
Impressed with power important for one's moment!

It was that Alberico Archinto went
To walk the library of Nöthnitz whose own motive
Was doubtless envy on the thought that so shelved
His own of one could draw men like this drew him.

Yes he would come to build his own library,
And some man much like this man superintend that,
Or he himself would do would he just tarry!

A steal might take place someday this to mean that
He Archinto was more esteemed than sorry,
And prouder just for this than such count when dead!

45

THE NUNCIO ARCHINTO
IMPRESSED WITH THE LIBRARIAN'S KNOWLEDGE

How know the fancies lurked in high-repressed men?
In wonder over how world facts seemed picked fruits,
And these to reach them swirled on stream delicious
Out of the mouth of erudition's sweet man,

He seemed no less in wonder over sick pain,
The outward suffering of Johann fixed close . . .
You dear soul said the nuncio with pinched lust,
I recommend a change of situation!

Archinto: You it seems suffer here, toil-wearied though pushed
To make ends meet, or stoke some dream in moonlit
Hours up to hunt for draw of bow's held-so thoughts!

Why not try Italy of mild clime for your bound health,
And there find much of art's food for your soul just,
And much of nature's for your recreation-strong self?

46

HE MEETS FATHER RAUCH,
THE JESUIT CONFESSOR OF THE KING OF POLAND

His long-time dream of Italy chance-took him
To say this was his own express desire's goal!
So nothing less these would commit to serve whole,
Till chance he showed ensconced from this plan spoken.

In their time Saxon Wittens ruled too Poland,
Which meant the Elector Poland's king could court hold
In Dresden or in Warsaw, the nuncio a virtual
Appointee to two cities though one role owned.

Invited to be frequent guest at Dresden,
Smiled Johann never failed to meet some Jesuits there,
In their time of that sort which was to meet in

The court of Romish nuncios place no matter!
Now Leopold Rauch confirmed that his belief won
He should in Rome find doubled his wealth made there!

47

HE ACQUAINTS IN LETTER TO CARDINAL PASSIONEI,
OWNER OF ONE OF THE WORLD'S GREAT LIBRARIES

Stirred Archinto introduced him to a third man
Of their long trust Domenico Passionei.
At present this deep-learned man was not only
The pope's friend but proud owner of some books important.

True of the self-drawn portrait's browed librarian,
Whose reservation put not one long over one nigh,
He Johann shed or pleaded both sides once he
Seemed more construed than wish could tend him for them.

One writing specimen based on the Greek world
Was sent this cardinal so pleased that his love hired
The German on condition theirs be faith shared!

More Father Rauch and Nuncio Archinto paired,
In their pursuit of him whose knowledge mattered
To their affair of heart wished that's spread outward!

48

A SIDE TRIP TO BRING HIS REUNION WITH PETER

He could postpone this or that thing he wished done,
Or this or that thing men else wished done for them,
But winter 1752 was certain
He could postpone no *more* their meeting wished on!

How long he waited while he wasted in such season,
To write or read of love hearts proved for dear them!
But his left drier-colder in desertion,
To reunite seemed heart's sole hope sole mission . . .

The teen boy he once offered light, shade, rootspace,
Was grown to be the aid and secretary
Of Colonel Retzow one of Potsdam's closest

In circle of the court of their king's merry.
To break once did inertia's bonds seemed now best!
He stepped down off the coach proud of the journey.

49

VIRGIN NO MORE TO POTSDAM

Although his Peter showed pleased on their meeting,
The sweet embrace seemed politic seemed less love!
How put this with his letters never let up
The sweet plead of their cause in each word's writing?

The bold strokes page-stood on received committing
Were once in personhood's stood presence held off . . .
Moods being of innuendo's press freed each up.
The visit occupied him three weeks' raced time,

The time too short to take his bearings when brought
So much to weigh from new experiences' new truths.
More settled seemed his Peter in court's teemed fold,

And surer of each strange connection took place:
To watch him soon emboldened Johann seen taught!
He wrote one friend the *rest* must word of mouth use.

50

HIS EXPERIENCE OF ALL-MALE LUST
IN THE COURT OF THE ABSOLUTE MONARCH FREDERICK THE GREAT KING OF PRUSSIA

The Europe which grew gossip knew how Frederick
Himself showed court the King of Prussia's crushes!
His strength in war feared, he could run his touches
On soldiers tolerant of his love's metric.

The great powers placed just versatile strik-
Ing men not mistresses in Potsdam's viewed sets,
To win the favor male plants won who most pleased
The great king's heart devoted to those sexed-like!

1752. Johann in Potsdam
Wrote I observe here Athens, Sparta, taste them,
And feel a reverence toward the great unstopped man.

Well Johann showed too *much* enthusiasm:
His gasps drew looks. I have endured more love than
I in the future will be shown I reason.

51

WINDING
DOWN IN THE COUNTRIFIED COURT OF NÖTHNITZ

His jovial mode went sometimes off the code's tone!
The parties of this Saxon count's court owned match
Of its things to the things of Potsdam's shown reach,
Although its moral likeness court wished not owned!

Once in the high-born's midst he rang in loud sound,
Mere turn could stop that . . . Silenus the count faced.
His jovial mode when self-dismissed still wound past
The guests, the servants, or the idlers brought round.

With them if shared tales of the Frederick seen loose,
The group was turned to mime drunk his superb love,
Till Heinrich's threats on Silenus such pranks bruised.

He faced the public sentence owed their world's mob,
And loss of writings meant to spare him time's cross!
He strove inside with night sweats, sleepless, torn up.

52

THE EMPOWERING CLIMAX OF HIS NIGHT SWEATS

How long faith counted on this count to show couth,
So stand to side with more men than proved cretins!
He misread lisp, highness, swishness in misreadings,
To see couth this mode-rococo count got up!

His signs of that the scolding proved were not proof,
Were emptiness itself, his spoiling's breached signs!
One old hen on the set of men's perceived strengths,
He owned each bitter wouse's mind rubbed cold off!

Still lived submitted to the wouse much-churned self,
Exposed to rumors, bound wrung should police raid,
Sunk in his room where just inked paper burned swift . . .

O expedite . . . O speed to publish . . .Own it this fate!
He took to lie in bed but drew strength storm-reefed,
And rose explosive through time's self-released wait!

53

JOHANN APPROACHES
IN A LETTER A PEN CONFIDANT BOUND TO AID HIM

He found peace writing one friend how trait no leave
Attends seems the important point which binds one.
The Muses tolerate inclined condition
And Reason which should mistrust instinct must step

In as their ally on this point to daunt one's posed self.
With mental reservation how deceive men?
One never does deceive the one *omniscient*
Almighty not Romish not Lutheran in grand motive!

Our instinct is the finger of the Almighty,
One first proof of his work the long-unleft trait.
You even I obey this since it is he!

Here till the time of Moses was the Law the Prophet.
Not the dead letter but the live heart needs me,
To own the help men mean would I theirs show faith!

54

THE SO SECRET USE OF HIM POSSIBLE TO THEM

Would Rome's faith Catholic faith exist to touch him,
Or would his knowledge touch Rome thus lent vision?
Would the triumvirate to court him think his mission
To show their peers their own truth overlooked then?

How was the too-near missed to owe men's custom?
Moved Passionei wrote he should outset on
The trip to Rome but be brought faith in Dresden.
The need was plain that in this man dwelt new men!

In Johann was deep learning mixed with strange lack
Of molding inhibition that Rome's classic
Inheritance seemed owned in mind that ranged back

To tell of themselves using time's elastic.
The male review on the Sistine stood void of impact,
Or Homer did Lucian did, once dulled its great clique.

55

COUNT VON BÜNAU COOL ON HEARING OF IT

To sense their plotting put such man's self on guard.
A show of faith should cause him blush if happened,
And leave him just one stuffed the nuncio's cabinet!
Instead he left their Dresden shier onward.

What would the count do when his hired dishonored
The Lutheran faith both shared to feel it saved them . . . ?
To lose the favor such count meant distressed mind,
And when he thought of this he thought of no word!

So word of his proposed conversion should use
A different mouth once Bünau should be told this.
A letter friend seemed right to brook the put news.

His correspondent wrote the count showed coldness.
Oppressed Johann: I thought him no real orthodox of closed views,
But there is how surprise ruins one's long-used nest!

56

COUNT AND WIFE OF HIM WARM IN TIME

At length once news lost novel punch the cool count
And countess said themselves in milder-found terms.
It drew from Johann wish to praise their sung charms
Up to the skies he took to bless minds both's crown!

Ecstatic Johann: To think both think in reason's sweet-revolved zone,
To find me no worse man despite their owned norms!
I wish to kiss the footsteps of their bound forms,
And promise I will serve for life souls thus shone!

Now Archinto put forth that his conversion
Should take place in mid-April though this saw him
Elude that date pretending strong need forced him

To meet the count in Dahl. But Rauch postponed then
Till June first in view of peer Jesuits' exertion
In preparation exercises Easter caused them.

57

HOW HE IS TO BE PAID LITTLE
YET LIVE HIGH TO OWE PASSIONEI OF THE BREVI

Just once his resignation was put in did
The nuncio disclose terms of his hiring!
The cardinal offered just three ducats per month,
Astounding Johann bitter in complaints said.

Then Archinto took pains that proved this same rate
Would do in cheap Rome so would seem a fortune,
And Rauch spoke for the Jesuits holding their man
Would earn a hundred guilders once the same faith!

On his arrival Passionei said he
Was to alight at no inn but alight there
At place of rooms to find his in the great See!

These were in his own palace opposite where
The pope lived, nearness requisite in that he
Was holder of the papal briefs long kept there . . . !

58

WORD OF PASSIONEI'S LIBRARY
IN HIS APARTMENT IN THE ROUND ABBATIAL CHURCH OF SAN BERNARDO ALLA TERME

He should leave naught to leave the count's library
Which he could not find present in one Passionei's,
So furnished in Greek manuscripts that from these
One could grow twice Greek Palaeography's tree,

The catalogue of Father Montfaucon's den sortie.
To hear this Johann wished trip's hour for conquest,
At least wished out of Dresden—place a point was
Made on the Rome most said he sought to marry.

He thought sure in own meantime he could live in
His friend's home—Peter still in swash town Potsdam—
But on he toiled in library indifferent.

He suffered from opinion of his soul's spawned
Disquietude, too from his Peter's being indifferent,
One he once molded like himself owed close bond!

59

HOW AS TO PETER HE LIVES TO OSCILLATE

At turns he said I feel restored through reason,
And let remembrance of him end extinguished!
I should show prudent in respect to friendships,
And no more tempt me to bear folly's passion!

But did he just receive his friend's best wishing,
It captivated him down to his being's depths!
I will support him since his father's strain leaves
Him wanting for the finer things this season . . .

Ah circumstances proved to grow some pain in
His new retirement—*he* would lead to hear needs
He stepped in so to meet that he maintain him!

Then on the swing he swore to end such using:
You with these Potsdam tricks do not deserve us,
Young Peter wishing him not seen in Potsdam!

60

DETACHMENT
TO DEEPEN HIS BOUND ATTACHMENT TO BOOKS

His love's loss was debilitating to him,
But in such times seems habit one's support-weight:
He discontinued social life but more did
His reading, writing, research through his soul's pain.

He paid no visits to the nuncio's den,
Abstained one Easter up to Easter a full year's tread,
1753 to 1754 hid
If read dear Homer three more times with close lean.

His refuge in the living Father Rauch lent,
But he did not confide his pain though this grew
Till he renounced him when on no more walks went!

To walk reminded him how frightful he now
Seemed in his solitude though still in books deemed
Himself to save if once should strike on just how.

61

HE MOVES IN WITH ADAM OESER AND HIS FAMILY

A friend is one's friend too once grows his most need.
His scenes for Hubertusburg nimbused bounced him,
Although pumped ceilings of the new Schloss Dahlen
Still drew some future dawn's commission owed that.

In 1754 he lived quite off site,
And hence would welcome Johann in his own home.
The burned-out lover down-timed in things common,
And moments let mere things support his coped head.

He could find faith in life or just distraction
To numb pain watching cheerful people's bustle,
To see it move who did show faith one watched them.

The jump on him was theirs in game or tussle,
Whose motion dazzled such slow mind till those went
Dulled down to bed when up to write rose who willed!

62

1754:
HE CONVERTS TO CATHOLIC FAITH IN THE REAL

In state of mind so pained he thought of what if.
He said what if the count die how should I fend?
The man who made no calls caused words to be sent
To Rauch directing him to find the nuncio's self

And tell him he was ready to take new faith.
The nuncio found great joy when brought this mind
Into the fold this his first one so high-grand,
And so in no time was brought up their sought date.

The close event took place in private chapel
With men in ritual robes to mime prescribed forms,
Set down of long duration's fix of great spell

The canons fixed of those Trent's and Pope Pius IV's.
He Johann, Archinto, two priests in sable,
And Rauch used signs to fit rite to life-wished course.

63

HOW HE EXPLAINS
HIS FINAL STEP IN A LETTER TO COUNT VON BÜNAU

A man once formed must not depart traits based on
Intrinsic wholeness without risk brought being's self;
So I should find departure from formed mind's well
A thing most difficult if so occasioned.

I prize deep friendships feeling formed to have one,
Or else find life void when such thing sublime's feel
Would be its best reward; how should I then fail
To take steps to secure this though with great pain?

The loftiest of lofty virtues friendship,
I mean not the smiled friendship Christians practice
Which is disinterested indifference in drift;

But mean their sort just few men of antiquity's best
Acquired for our design; this faith change means life
And based on principle I change mine quite pleased.

64

HOW STILL IN
HIS SAME LETTER HE FALLS AT FEET OF THE COUNT

At feet of him the count he fell who showed moved,
And not just pleased he now thought to entreat him.
Your Excellency ones great know not this friend-
Ship's sort since it requires renouncing most's love,

And shrinks not from compounding solitude's truth
Of rumor, misery, age, death up to ridding.
Still I entreat you of the mind enlightened,
The eye to use in like of Deity whose proof

Is most ourselves when look on us through level
Aplomb seeing all tongues, nations, sects, creed-users
To constitute ourself though free from evil . . .

So he now thought to plead the count this no worse,
And ventured that reward would find his great self,
The merciful self wished in so blessed owned course.

65

A MIDSUMMER SMALL EDITION
TO PREFIGURE THE DECEMBER NUMBER-DEEP ONE

He raised himself up deemed to publish somewhere
His book of self-original Thoughts so-penned
On Imitation. He knew how great it was when
Obscure to men should welcome its caused summer.

It was from hot midsummer to September
His spirit took the published path his Thoughts went.
It owed men solid in ideals that most in
The shadow bigots threw showed lent depths honor.

Just 50 copies printed of his penned work,
He sent prospective patrons Thoughts like true gold
To shine on minds-in gifts of times past since lurked.

It was a start propitious start of book sold
In copies thousands deep to grow his fame stark,
December's Dresden printing boosted through cold!

66

AT LAST WINCKELMANN PUBLISHES HIS THOUGHTS:
THOUGHTS ON THE IMITATION OF GREEK WORKS IN PAINTING AND SCULPTURE

On heights was said that one to mock reversed then!
One else defended him repeating his part!
1755. A riddle too if wise work,
He published his time-long-in-work excursion,

Thoughts on the Imitation of Greek Works in
Fine Painting and Fine Sculpture. His comprised art?
A treatise, then a feigned attack on this work,
Then a defense from that of principles filled part one.

His person certain writer of the first part,
His second part used someone's different voicing,
And someone's different still else took the third part!

His part-first voice *pure*, then one's pompous chosen,
And then one's neutral-sounding inswept art's sort,
Each so-contributed showed thirded Thought's mind.

67

WINCKELMANN'S DICTUM:
THE WAY FOR US TO BECOME GREAT EVEN INIMITABLE IS TO IMITATE THE ANCIENTS

His work won praise for views that stirred discussion
In the artistic circles men of name used.
His Thoughts on Imitation made him famous,
The work reprinted, translated, and passed men . . .

In unexpected liege was Fuseli shown
The English translator, Gothic painter though was!
More classic Goethe sensed his mind expand most,
To see his leanings worded in the mused tome.

His Thoughts contained first mention of the doctrine
Developed in each work of his the ideal,
Defined as being that which for one looking

Holds noble simplicity to join calm grandeur.
To own this bound one path's use to thought vital,—
Stirred imitation of the ancients' manner.

68

1755:
HE OUTSETS ON THE WELL-SUPPLIED JOURNEY TO ROME

On feel of new life his new faith put in them,
His patrons lobbied the great man Augustus
To pension Johann . . . Saxon Elector he was,
And King of Poland from this period Witten,

He thought inside that he could feel a heel in
The failure to reward such merit's cause thus
To grant to him two hundred thalers' just use . . .
The great news of his lobbiers' success went

To clinch the hope he felt the hour he outset.
So having published his Thoughts there in Dresden,
He took the trip to Rome the costs provided

On 80 ducats of a pouch Rauch reached him.
In join of Master Roos the royal butler's Jesuit
Son he went in a post-coach plied with rich wine.

69

WINED,
DINED, AND STUCK BLISTERED IN AUGSBURG

He clung views Cheb to Trent on rocking motion
In wind past towns . . . Upper Palatinate's Amburg
And Regensburg went rolled to old town Neuburg
On river Danube, each of these towns stopped in

To be received with sumptuous-lived smoothing
In Jesuit-college dens stocked for the men served.
He made gifts to each host but best was Neuburg
Where Rector Ligeritz paid visits whose themed

Two perched on bed to share jokes taking life on.
He Johann left his luggage there when on foot
Went seven miles to Augsburg blisters creeping;

Although spent eight days more than fond could,
Since Jesuits dispersing to their Italian-
Obtained provincials used each coach of one did!

70

HE TASTES THE ALPS THEN ON TASTES VENICE

His letter sent one friend praised all things Tyrol.
Escape from Augsburg brought to pad one carriage
A man, wife, and two of the marriage furnished
As well as a castrato bless his dear soul,

He Johann passed through luscious nature's mural,
Each Bozen's, Brixen's, Innsbruck's, Trento's, Mestre's,
Astonished to observe the high peaks near-pressed
Till even went the route down to fix shore's sprawl.

What then see? Venice loom up near the chopped waves.
Johann in His Own Words: A path runs in the loftiest ranges like in
A chamber one walks while each half-hour up leaps

At base of some mount's fearful beauty each inn,
Its beds as present as some town's though none is
To see where springs such provender for reaching.

71

HE SORTS ALL THE TEEMING MEMORIES OF TRIP

The guests like of a whole town just road gives birth.
The square unseen a feast is forked on silver,
Wrote Johann to one friend thus brought to dinner
In Bozen, Comburg, Innsbruck perched in high mirth.

Johann on Venice: Town Venice disconcerts one's first look which forth
Of that hush-waits on mind till thoughts grow finer;
One's mind upset for how begs logic this mere
Dream of a town this comes to share the right world.

On Traveler Johann: Zanutti the librarian was not found;
To tour San Marco's library was thus missed.
On water to Bologna storm could not drown

One who the crazed castrato said slept through this!
In churches in or near Bologna brought round,
He looked on paintings connoisseur should hold rich.

72

ROME

The road to lead him went slow through the country.
It went from hill to hill succeeding with slow *un*wind.
Each dropped behind like the spent veil of someone
To house veiled till the moment it caused bound sigh . . .

Now neared the view each hilltop of stones run high,
Left walls, great forts, intents turned ruins rounding
The lived-in dwellings, solid churches round-domed . . .
How picturesque on green great stones of Rome lie!

Tone monuments spare monuments stood cornered
And let the tile-roofed house or castle groups stream
In top-tilt counterpoint drawn with the turned world.

The road if joined outspread to find the whole scene,
A dome's blue cusps to meet horizons where shared
With giants the place founts filled in disrobed dream!

73

ENSCONCED IN ROME,
YET A MISUSED HAND FOR THE FAITHFUL'S CONSUMPTION

True tawdriness, wretchedness, uncleanliness were
Increased with sensed distress in the waste regions
About Rome though here he was in his rich friend's
Sprawled palace well-perceived each wall or figure!

He ended in praise of Passionei's nature,
Whose candor drew on him the rest's impatience,
Whose firmness caused slip in detractors' presence,
Whose rectitude was still acknowledged each hour

In place where vice and virtue were concealed right
Beneath men's policy and hypocrisy rife.
His real embrace of Romish faith was still quite

Deficient he would note in things which blessed life,
To wit when made sign of the cross not his right
But left hand went thrust in front of his watched self!

74

A LIBRARIAN ALIVE TO THE STIMULUS OF BOOKS,
AND TWO LIBRARIES TO EQUIP HIM WITH ROOMS

To take the grant from Dresden brought him income;
200 thalers smoothed Elector-used thoughts.
His *spirit* used some other means like statues,
And living ones seen lush in streets-combined Rome.

He occupied his first chore to describe some:
Apollo Belvedere named-such court's housed choice,
Laocoön, Antinous, Belvedere Torso utmost
Of ancient sculpture's triumphs the scribe mentioned.

Year two of stay his limit, his plans stood changed,
Once burst was home's peace in the Seven Years' War.
Step in the Cardinal Passionei whose most-ranged

Library needed him; Archinto lived returned there,
Now Cardinal Archinto whose goal draw up clinched
Of library in need, either in his corner.

75

ARCHINTO'S STEPS
UP TO ENRICHED VICE-CHANCELLOR OF THE HOLY SEE

Aged to his middle twenties Archinto entered
The Curia—the central body which for pontiffs
Administers the power of their bishop's office
And which groups of a number of skilled men serve

To run the church to corners of the seen world—
In 1724 . . . Years on once become priest,
He was Archbishop of Nicea though this
Mere title let him serve grand court to grand court

As nuncio first in Tuscany then in Poland.
On his return in 1754 this
Astute man turned the governor of Rome

And Vatican Vice-chamberlain, thus the treasury's
Wise overseer. Deemed papabile he drew some
Votes in the early ballots though saw cheered else.

76

ROOMS IN THE STUDIO MENGS'

High were the lofty ideals which love brought things;
His notion of the requisites of writing
And notion of the requisites of living
He formed on one sense conscious of their true links.

In Rome such numbers of the great raised up springs
It caused one to disown first stir to wish in,
More to consider how create whose being
Saw no men though with the exception owed Mengs

Who for their excellence shown learning honed skills
Looked long into the inner depth of true art.
His living options thence obtained some rooms else,

Now welcome in the studio took brush forth.
The need some measure of own talents joined selves,
To weigh relations, set deportment, be brought birth.

77

HIS LIVING-MATE ANTON MENGS

Dutch clubs connected Dutchmen, German German,
And Austrian Austrian once members flocked Rome.
Too letter post connected men whose brooks-shone
States flowed ideal in fame-shaped spring of person.

Too court-life went to join not leave men searching!
His dwelling-mate when first he dwelt in walked Rome
Was Anton Mengs world's painter sweet to look on!
Aid to his friend's he grew from his friend's learning.

Mengs was the tester of him, was the endued stream,
Was vehicle to spread their concepts through worlds,
Was conduit to sweep new research of them.

One's brushful touch would join one's studious torch,
And visions formed between them burn to stop time
In the eternal ideal lifts the true arts.

78

WINCKELMANN'S
SUBLIME EKPHRASIS ON APOLLO BELVEDERE

He not the first man who found male-on art great,
He found Apollo in a space brooked "heightened",
To mean placed in it was a long-deemed-high thing,
Sensed to excite no first love since was first made.

He recognized its fame for which life's world paid
The books-in compliment print, plate, engraving!
He neared it with his chest grown full from breathing,
As if to near it more breaths did male heart need!

He was to make it possible to view this
Male beauty not for art achievement but for itself,
Since wrote of that experience of who feels!

Sense-deep Johann: I feel expand chest so lets soul receive well,
And uplifts so I grow with him whose mood swells
With brilliance-owned embodiment of life's male!

79

LIFE IMITATES ART

He was to give the sculpture life through young men,
Who said he sought ones hearing him speak on love,
Ones rotated once life took his loves long off,
A new soul to find blond, young, handsome, Roman!

His roommate Peter was turned Mengs dear Anton,
Who pupil in Mengs' form Franz Stauder wound up!
Franz Nicoló Castellani turned soon up,
And Friedrich von Berg turned soon up in handsome,

As though replacement-long for Friedrich surnamed
Von Bülow. Livonian von Berg the final
One to conform to his ideal due world's fame

Was turned one else but who was doomed to end vile.
So praise von Berg the sensitive to art's men,
Swank-suave, long-limbed, well-doing in his fine self.

80

A FRIENDSHIP OPENS WITH CARDINAL ALBANI
AS HIS LIVING OPTIONS TEND USE OF TWO PALACES

One's fame went to produce more letter friendships.
A correspondence with Firenze's Baron
Von Stosch would bring a recommendation for him,
On strength of which he entered on a deemed-best

Acquaintance with one from Rome's placed Albanis.
With Alexander Albani dining or then
With Passionei he re-willed his patron
Once nuncio now cardinal these peer-men matched.

The trait pride left him rooms in either's palace,
In Archinto's who lived returned there in Rome,
In Passionei's who swept from Rome if sat pleased.

In either's he was the library's man found,
In Palace of the Brevi or in the Cancellaria's peace,
The purpose of arranged books keeping him roomed . . .

81

ETERNAL-CITY NOISE
AND EXCITEMENT-HIGH NIGHTS IN WORLD-WEARY ROME

He now went home betimes since it induced health,
Was early to rise, was early to bed, renounced plays
And operas sometimes witnessed in his young days,
And slept whole-undisturbed nights in resolve's self.

He slept midst of long-empty palace rooms shelved
To hold the treasures grown deep of minds on quest.
The town quite quiet in most hours' hot-shone days,
Rome was in nights the Devil let loose through Hell!

It was to owe men's freedom which was found there,
Or men's neglect of their policing ones ranged
In brawling, shooting, lighting firework or bonfire . . .

Insightful Johann:　So growth-fixed populace grows up untamed sense,
All magistrates wearied of the banishings sounder,
All magistrates wearied of the men's rope-hangings.

82

1756:
PYGMALION DOES A TURN IN LUDOVISI GARDEN

In spring one sense-expands love since survives time
The winter owned to spread death in the field earth!
His budding lust outdrew his will to sail forth
And have Frascati, Tivoli, and like towns sweep him!

In Ludovisi villa's space Pygmalion
Stepped up for posed inspection of some swell work.
He wished some chisel-fixed of strokes to be neared,
And gripped the stone here then there to up-lift him.

Once tiring from such grip without breathed life thus
To ease embrace of thing love studied heart-moved,
He sought to dismount when stone fell in great crush.

He brushed himself off but inside preserved thought
Of writing On the Restoration of Sculpt' Statues . . . ,
Be this with Letters from Rome *never* there wrought.

83

MAURICE THE PRINCE OF ELBOEUF
DISCOVERS HERCULANEUM BELOW MODERN PORTICI IN CAMPANIA NEAR NAPLES

To dig a well to quench a planned home's new thirst,
The Prince d'Elboeuf discovered homes below earth.
His workers dug down–down–to town time lowered,
The Herculaneum Vesuvius parched.

The tunnel dug went straight to find without search
A statue to extract raised up off toil's start.
The prince soon put more funds into the proud work
Of raising Roman treasures up to sunburst.

But better for the sculptures than the book-scrolls,
To deem were carbonized logs stacked for fuel needs,
So burned for torches to up-light who looked fools!

The first to drop his carried logs met one's streaks
Of writing on the dark-charred crumbled chalk's folds,
Ink black on black though visual like that one reads.

84

THE SPANISH BOURBON CHARLES III
AND THE ROQUE HIS ENGINEER OF EXTRACTION

The king of the Two Sicilies Charles III took
The site on who chose Roque de Alcubierre,
To engineer the dig neared military.
The work was done for vain's cause Charles to see stock

His house with finds that high minds' interest this woke.
A house d'Elboeuf built caused the queen wish there be
A residence in town Portici where she
And Charles might summer passing treasures if walked

Their rooms of items guests discussed on through space.
The military operation's real tone
Was of a treasure hunt spread tunnels brought reach . . .

D'Elboeuf's finds Johann saw when still in Dresden,
Although trekked to Portici with bound thoughts raised,
To tell of that unearthed for men's enrichment.

85

1757:
IN NAPLES AND ALL PLACES

Assumed were character traits thought for matching
The men he met whose will could cool-discern them:
To the museum's master self-important
He strove to seem mere simpleton head-scratching!

The queen's confessor was this master's great friend
And served in concert with him once concerned him:
To this owed the denied reception their queen
Would show him till he spoke of such ill-based thing!

To learned of archaeologists he was modest;
To their robust of toilers he showed sweet depths;
To the proud man Tanucci rich in knowledge

He strove to seem sincere in thankful-deemed steps;
To women quiet in curiousness he was honest;
To pompous spouts he showed his looks in thin drifts.

86

HE SEES PAESTUM
AND HEARS OF HARMONIOUS NATURE IN GESSNER'S IDYLLS

Trip-bound companions Johann, chamberlains two
Of the king's from Cologne, one Johann Volkmann
Of Hamburg, mixed-in travelers, liveried foot-men,
And boat-men pad the scene so to command view!

In spread from Naples these take towns of scene so
Said in the mouth Pozzuoli, Baiae, Misenum rolling
To Cumae of the Sibyl time's' vie-deathless woman,
And lush Caserta crowned house point for span too

Of a great aqueduct Saint Peter's in height.
The group see Paestum's Doric-order temples,
And in a boat on swept Salerno's lent bight

Hear Volkmann sound one Solomon Gessner's Idylls.
These stress the sentiment of people when sweet,
And sing the picturesque life without human ripples.

87

1757 TO 1758:
ABOUT HIS CONNECTION TO PHILIP VON STOSCH

One baron of Firenze Philip von Stosch
Developed friendship with him willed through letters.
He it was introduced one like of great peers
Since deemed important-to-him patron shown trust,

As spare Albani proved to be when idle-owned much.
Now died this Stosch on reaching 66 years
Of age in home to house gems cut with pictures,
Incised gems which stole breath to lie one down dust.

One Visitor to Stosch: He strips down Italy, holds her in submission,
Unwilling to give up to else one sole prop,
Although will show else worlds of props oppressing!

One final-hour request was *he* should draw up
A criticism-based book of intaglios these seen
In numbered thousands of them owed his love's truth.

88

1758 TO 1759:
ABOUT HIS CONNECTION TO MUZEL VON STOSCH

The dead's request was stressed for one his nephew's
Appeal would bring to see in life these housed things.
Two thousand five hundred ancient gems in housings
He should describe if suit will of the dead Stosch . . . !

In life Stosch wrote on posh gems, drawings, statues:
As proper archaeologist he used sense
But *never* learned parsed beauty's truth in told things,
One did concluded later of his late use.

Installed in his great-sized rooms each one looped in,
Here Johann toiled for six months for engraved gems
To enter criticism's index of them.

His unrelenting toil was done with cadence,
Although more struck the news to interrupt him,
How in Rome Archinto passed, Muzel to read winced.

89

ARCHINTO DEAD OF POSSIBLE POISONING,
AND THE WAR SUED BETWEEN PRUSSIA AND SAXONY

He lost one patron, the Cancellaria's rooms,
And that part of himself which shared one dead's life!
He earlier forewent a post so that left
A needier learned man some means on cash sums . . .

Once learned war moved the Prussians on the Saxons
He thought of Peter thought of him in sad self.
He earlier forewent a pension that if
His country suffer he should share that's faced wants.

His "I" saw Lamprecht though was torn between two
Moods sad for rippled Saxony but not up
To wish cruel Prussia punished when meant him too!

Tender Johann: I weep in heart for that place I was brought up,
But feel fear for the safety of a friend who
Attends the crusher of the miles deep thoughts loved.

90

I:
THE VILLA ALBANI PARNASSUS FRESCO BY ANTON MENGS

The theme though was each master's re-stood so his,
It seemed no other's now such right one blessed took.
The theme much waited to reward whose self looked
Deep on the visions Herculaneum's thought stressed,

In figures moved Parnassus' sort should hold pleased,
As pictured themselves in the soulful wealth brooked!
Mere composition's use holds each in depth touched,
As soul's toil does in nearness to see wrought blessed

Of sun the sober light compared forms' cause neared,
So counted nine's works measured off the brightness.
The creed exists for those who leave the least's world,

To give mind use of arts which let needs seek depths!
It should disclose men in supports sun stretched forth
Shone to show how obtain their time-enriched selves.

91

II:
THE VILLA ALBANI PARNASSUS FRESCO BY ANTON MENGS

Would seen-mnemonic prop join their mind-rich lives,
It would group like of memoried selves join *pure* skills.
It helps remembrance to put nine of theirs each
In one arts-strong house of the cause-compelled sibs!

Zeus sired on Memory's or Mnemosyne's sex
The daughters who lived stirred in nine of arts' selves:
Vocations purest in walk's categories
Were nine in number like their daughters skilled each.

Except to live environed through these wrought nine,
One lives the life dumb might seeks in dumb servants
Each to submit to some stand power brought time.

He paints the creed owes just inspired works' persons,
A cardinal's rule to use Apollo's of men
More put in order one's self which brings world sense!

92

PASSIONEI DEAD OF OLD AGE,
ON RETIRING TO A CAMALDOLESE MONASTERY NEAR FRASCATI OUTSIDE ROME

His use to Passionei found growth, peak, decline too,
More ebb for this man's death than Archinto's death.
The great achievement brought himself did owe self,
But this he owed his patrons in the time grew.

So much self-present drew from the two men's flew!
He sat remembering the recent one's life,
A nobleman who from thirteen in Rome dwelt,
And Plato read in Collegio Clementino,

And law in La Sapienza, soon the secretary
To relative Filippo Gualterio, cardinal,
Made envoy, nuncio, bishop, cardinal though he early

Took a retirement when his source he mourned well,
To work composing music in no hurry,
Twelve deep sonatas published for memorial . . .

93

HOW LIKE IS CHANGE

The under-librarian to Angelo Quirini
Was fit to run the Holy See's Library.
On Cardinal Quirini's death who else would there be?
Passionei would succeed him like Albani

Succeed Passionei these things passed between the
Dear friends of Johann's just observed to serve high!
It seemed that nothing changed for the library-
Room benefits he drew on through own-gained See.

Since then he could read on his friendships in books,
To donate to the Vatican if men would!
Someday it might be possible to own things in such!

Yet till then theirs were secret plots to minds vowed,
Up from deep childhoods to live different in touch
So bettered this world's men on sex of them sought!

94

HOW TO MISS MENGS
SMARTS HIM DESPITE HIS ENJOYMENT OF TRANQUILITY

He mourned one second friend to lose this summer
Of 1761 this friend Mengs who set
Out with his family to Madrid where would lead
A life on high in Charles III's honor.

As Solomon Gessner wrote him Mengs lost no tear;
All seemed prone to construe him happier traveled.
Yet Johann wrote him easier untraveled
To own peace undisturbed the peace joy owns dear.

Johann: Our lives begin to be rich once impetuous
Desires diminish though begin to be poor
Once our possessions grow deep: I believe such

Is mine to live to die but die to live more!
Mengs was not happy in Spain but left his thoughts
In Rome to time his feet touched on art's rich shore.

95

STRESS ON THE IDEAL IMITATION
AND THE SUBLIME-IDEAL ARTIST MENGS WAS STRENGTHENED TO BE

Mengs let him realize his ideas for art's cause,
Since he of artists saw that when he bid these
To picture his stance on the path of greatness,
He meant these imitate retaining their choice

Of artful handling of the art's matched virtues.
He welcomed more than copies to call slavish,
Since what is imitative still bears shaped traits
Original in reason's, spirit's, matter's pure use,

So might rise into own unique-deemed nature
And art take form from nature's individual,
As proof of different contexts if retraced sure . . .

Mengs stood embodier become one's best real
Sign of the ideal's blessing thence for better
Touched artists when attempted that's revival!

96

HE LIVES TO SPLIT TIME
BETWEEN ALBANI'S PALACE IN ROME AND HIS VILLA ON THE VIA SALARIA

Soon Cardinal Albani wrote to offer
Him four rooms in his palace two which looked down
On gardens ancient statues marked for walking.
His own Passione's library's brother,

This promised reading to each sleeping-brought hour.
He need not trouble but needs of shelved books tend,
And put in time if possible for token
Of friendship would friend join with friend to supper.

The choice of space seemed one to give him peace so
To help his study in the quiet's world used.
Such residence in Rome was to repeat too

In Via Salaria's rooms which stood like-purposed,
Since over, under, or sides-near his kept few
Dwelt no one in rooms else, found empty their views!

97

A LIBRARIAN TO ALESSANDRO ALBANI

Outside or in Rome: His third time's being librarian for books lent
Him Alessandro Cardinal Albani's own home.
The Porta Salaria villa wound round
Antiquities in stood collection's posed blend.

Here or in travel Johann studied choice thing
And thing of sculpture treasures seen for Roman.
Acquiring sense of ancient art though owned none,
He was unrivaled for his self-instruction.

His observation method joined deep research,
To let him hold identified the copies
The Roman copies of Greek art the real source.

His times first held that Roman remnants showed best
The high achievement of antiquity's works,
But he showed their conceptions owed Greek models!

98

ALBANI'S STEPS
UP TO ENRICHED ENVOY IN TALKS WITH SAVOY

At age nine he was made in name a member
Of Rome's Knights of Saint John to start preparing
Him for a military path. His person
At fifteen was made colonel for the same's cheer!

His "weak sight" unpropitious, his path changed for
The clergy under guidance found unerring
Of uncle-to-him pope . . . Yet Innocent XIII
It was made him a cardinal. Earlier his manner

Would suit him as a diplomat to receive kings,
Or to retain the pope's rights to some countries,
Or to restore possessions lost from seethings.

Yet he could be soft over rights to one else
Acquired through might if on concession rich things
It brought the envoy, abbacy of some bells.

99

TWO LAZZI:
GEORGE AND FILLIP LAÇI, SOLDIERS OF ALBANIA

The rich walk the same earth the used poor walk too.
Aristocrats ease just the path theirs own best.
Italian history of the Albanis
Owes two swell brothers George and Fillip who drew

Up in the town Urbino just once both flew
Their service in the war between those countries
Albania and Venice . . . In times that found these
Allegiance-minded pimps right for pelf's choice few—

In points combined the faith with countries lives hold—
The two impressed with diplomatic skill-sets
And shrewdness-showing politics when reached out!

Both lent the church and government their rich wiles
As managers who thrived to mean their breed would
Still reach out so these two worlds grew up fit selves!

100

DESCENDANT OF THEM ALESSANDRO
AS PATRON, COLLECTOR, AND CULTURAL CAPITALIST

One in their legal mold from prudence showed wise
At La Sapienza something thence stood drawn on,
Although developed powers for antiquarian
And arbiter of taste in stone-limbed bodies.

His passion felt for ancient-world art noticed
Youth up this swelled support of digs all round Rome.
The findings he acquired he lent important
Weight then used these for favor's gifts or sold these

To fund his living on a grand scale least seen—
Although the German Johann shared this times wry.
His first apprenticeship for this art action

Was served beneath the papal antiquary
Whose function of some tedium would precede him,
The name his Marcantonio Sabatini.

101

ALBANI AS A SPY
TO BREED THE LIBERTY OF THE ENGLISH

Own double-dealing suits the one of skilled heights,
In diplomatic politics of climbed moves.
A climber switches ends shown looks that men toss,
To bottom-draw their sight-run trust in high liege.

The pope's own envoy who was formed capricious
Opposed him who housed for a guest the one Scotch
Who exiled claimed the British throne just Rome was
Deemed unified to wish one Catholic saw reached.

But practiced in the reset of men's sexed selves,
As stood in Rome's midst antique art put these new,
He here moved to receive from one of spies else

The Jacobite plans for invasion's reached coup:
The notes John Chute took sent the English whistles,
The Jacobite hopes were then theirs to sweep low!

102

THE VILLA ALBANI

The house now lived in housed his friend's collection,
One he co-curated for great antiquities' reach.
The plan of 1743 was realized
As finished stage in 1763's time.

Architect Carlo Marchionni was the lead one,
Although Giovannis Nolli of map's brightness
And Piranesi of mind's prisons due some real states
Were second architects for the enriched plan.

High-ceilinged rooms, double-height interior loggia,
And terraced steps meant this house was a stage first
To host for antiquarians balls of caused glow.

Mengs' painting of Parnassus poured in vault's burst,
And Antinous leaned from a relief which looks drew,
As did one tempietto's "ruins" which brought search!

103

THE ZENITH YEARS OF WINCKELMANN

Albani put him forth. Pope Clement XIII
Appointed Johann Vatican-wise Scriptor
And Prefect of Antiquities some livelier,
In charge of manuscripts be if in German.

His Letter to Bianconi bound important
Art insights in form used for the Elector-
Al Prince and Princess Saxon either ever
His to invigorate on studies Tour-Grand.

His triumph 1764 drew present:
His History of Ancient Art of great praise
Tied art to rise, peak, fall of civilization.

His An Attempt at Allegory saw reached
His Secret Monuments of Antiquity seen
To warrant Preliminary Treaty's preface.

104

ITEMS ON HIS SCHEDULE

Twice each week of his schedule were sweet parties.
He then stood near the cardinal in their grand home,
To host those nobles of life's sex deemed handsome
And sex deemed fair some even seen quite peerless.

Too introduced were strangers those the sort's best.
He met on evenings more men come to stand round
In their friend Countess Cheroffini's grand home,
She who looked on it well since her time's pure bliss.

Twice each week of his schedule he dined when met
With Passionei though the great man was not easy
With the Albanis' product . . . Still it was sense made

The art greet charmed stares, carriages stand ready,
Nettuno summer them, nights Mediterranean wait,
And Castel-Gandolfo's space sweep Theresa Albani!

105

HIGH-EXQUISITE EVENINGS AT CASTEL-GANDOLFO

To Castel-Gandolfo place seen beautiful he
Accompanied the cardinal and the princess . . .
The rig went rolled through country seeming endless,
And time went eased that stuffs rose up for ones free.

One's sister Princess Theresa Albani,
In hidden times she rumored lots to stain this
Man thought her rival for inheritance ties,
If still between the two friends' trust stepped no she!

On seem materialized the help of change that
The Landgrave of Hesse-Cassel gained ear if be
The post then vanished with posts wished in Wien did.

Still sumptuous life revolved here or there each sigh
The horn more spilled when then who could sustain it,
Who but some prince of Civitella-Cesi?

106

THE TORLONIA,
PRINCELY FAMILY OF CIVITELLA-CESI OF ROME

His worries would end if he took the tonsure,
And let friends mediate to bring him formed means.
Still how to let death come could means secure since
The life or place he loved when then lived on there?

Someday the family Torlonia would come there,
And be replacements of the first importance
To the Albani, Johann, even dear Mengs
Shown to live on in place he brushed art's wonder . . . !

So means some would find who like those Albani
Once reached out thus to help men's great caprices
Of church and government the greatest ones be!

The same acquired theirs in the times when its wise
Administered the finances of one See,
The Vatican whose pope's wealth let those with ties.

107

1762:
THE TOUR GUIDE OF ROME MEETS A NEW LOVE

Among those strangers he was bound to guide well
In Rome's stage of a Grand Tour high-bred men took
Was Berg this Friedrich R. von Berg on one look
His love for life since proof for taste his sight dwelt.

Berg's stay in Rome was short in time though he felt
Obliged when post request was made in tensed talk.
To mail owed those things read in letter-thin brook,
As Johann opened up his heart through scribe's spell.

Expressive Johann: You in your face and figure in your mood and spirit
Attracted me caused from the first more ruled sense.
You traced the harmony transcending mere need,

Attuned from that eternal chord which holds things
In perfect union, how on use-long merit
A body sentiment formed joined such soul's springs.

108

HE GUIDES THE DOUR OWNER OF ALL MARYLAND

His guide role turned chore grew his burnt reluctance,
Once found discerned in *some* less sense for beauty.
Lord Baltimore was shown such Tour though not he
Who then owned all of Maryland showed *much* sense,

To find no more to love in Rome than those things
Most stood to mind Saint Peter's or Apollo's body.
All too formed in the same set mold were those three
The feeling for the beautiful scarce brought minds

The Duke of Gordon, brother of him, and Lord Hope.
Young were the ones to keep him on guide's sure path;
The Prince of Mecklenburg-Strelitz was a dear youth

Of seventeen on Tour's end pupil for a year's drift;
The Prince of Brunswick on Rome's stage of Europe
Sought him for guide, Brunswick Akhilleus there met.

109

THE APPRECIATIVE AND THE UNAPPRECIATIVE
HEAR HIM USE THE LOFTIEST WORDS AND IMAGES

Ones old were owed the Tour more men like English
Ambassador Lord Hamilton the one sent
To Naples a great eye for figures owning,
Lord Stormont the Ambassador sent those Viennese,

Chum recommended on his earned seat John Wilkes,
Or on pelf Frenchmen Desmarest called bon homme
And Rouchefoucault called of himself a grand one,
Although the sights were grander in the guide's nest.

Appreciative men bettered his Tour skill-set,
And clapping was not frowned on were it soft-couth.
Appreciativeness helped restore who wilted,

Some Baltimore of thirty scarce the soft youth
To sit in carriage sour-unsmiled when still smiled
His guide who strove to tell of sights the most loved!

110

MISTER BOOTH THE NAME IS JOHN WILKES

Times sooner than supporters of him died shot;
Or he earned rights to print debates for printers,
Or he proposed that bill reforming theme's first,
Or he supported rebels whose bid fight brought

American Independence; or he wished fought
The ones so scorned the Papist Act cold cinders
To leave the Popery Act something seen worse,
To mark a turning-point opinion's list showed;

That voters whose rights he won to decide those
Who were to represent them rather than deem
The House of Commons to decide for its choice,

Were lent his leave to vote out just the man him
Who once rushed to oppose the Jacobite cause;
He was a strong voice of the Parliament's scene.

111

A PRINCE OF DESSAU IN NEED:
HOW COMPASSION MENTORS HIM ON A NIGHT

One reached his rooms one evening without escort-
Attendants or sword when looked to demand both!
So with just traveler's staff in his loose hand's chuff,
A high-bred form-great man put with his said word

That he was from Dessau who wished to be learned,
And needed help since a most-sheltered man-youth.
He settled down with presence though remained up
To midnight both brought vimful tears to shed forth . . . ,

So humble seemed his willing self should be taught.
Johann on the Prince: The Prince of Anhalt-Dessau looks formed of nature
To seem great friend and citizen though exalts that

On strength of birth, shape, and captivating feature.
His condescension joins a humble trait that
To do bad is impossible for this heir!

112

THE IDLY AMIABLE BARON OF DAHLBERG, CANON

A sign times else to mean the being mind-upclosed,
A title causing him to set his bristles,
The canon of Mayence was more than said his
Ecclesiast norm was thought one who posed depths.

His taste showed sense for things of beauteous use,
And nature wrought him for effect though this was
A thing in turn used when wished his effect pressed
So moved the peer let to observe him through such

Amiable, perceptive, willed-to-learn self.
Aesthetic in his form he it seemed found more
One in the likeness of himself showed charmed male.

Once home in Germany to bring guide's honor,
He promised him to learn Greek, baron formed-well
Von Dahlberg who was canon though like *none* were.

113

IN LOVE
WITH THE NOBLE LIVONIAN FRIEDRICH VON BERG

One handsome, well-read, leisured, sensitive-souled
To form male beauty, mentored, swash companion,
Young Friedrich R. von Berg was new love's lent man,
A nobleman born to inspire one he ruled,

With Johann dedicating to him words which he called
His On the Nature and the Cultivation
Of Sensibility to Beautiful Art tending
The pen-formed chord between this and his gifts full.

The Papal Antiquary, writer, conductor
Of self-high tourists in the Eternal City,
Much Johann wooed him though considered luckier,

To know from opposite gaze such with pressed sigh!
Berg stood it for a time though then struck off for
The Paris one earned on wealth's rise to heights free!

114

HOW HIS 1762 LETTER ON DISCOVERIES
PUT THE DIG ON BETTER FOOTING TO EARN HIM THE TITLE FATHER OF SCIENTIFIC ARCHAEOLOGY

Time still stands Johann in the scene of then's world
Beside the son nineteen of Count von Brühl blessed!
His Letter on Discoveries soon published,
Addressed to von Brühl, willed the public mind court-

Ed in form let the private zone feel entered.
He criticized Alcubierre's knowledge
Of art as neared the moon's of-lobsters knowledge,
And roasted methods that took dug of mines forth.

His chief concern seemed how preserved art objects:
He stood rebuked men's melting down of fragments
Of six bronze horses to cast one whole of these,

And stood rebuked men's cutting out wall paintings,
To be in frames moved from in-situ focus.
He stands beside the count's son sighed for leanings.

115

THE SOUL OF THE DIGS

His times looked some to rumble with lot-strewn digs,
The deep-dug pits with things exhumed from sleeping.
Dirt-swum stone to connect with book lore steeped-in
Seemed each hour on the cusp of view to thought rich . . .

A whiff of newness struck some drunk for new whiffs,
And earth seemed heaving with lots to bequeath men.
How was his interest formed for men's pits with lean
Of him on over their things raised for who stretched?

Those things to be unearthed with rumble he mused
Were not just things but were men's souls things hid in,
Souls things could re-strike long since in real life used.

The jump was his who long perceived through reading
The ancient context of the unearthed richness,
As things found souls his come to help men see them!

116

1763:
HE IS MADE A LIBRARIAN OF THE HOLY SEE

Although no diocese he ruled he was named under-
Librarian in charge of one whole section
Of Vatican Library this owned like some
Possession just a prince ruled shown men's wonder.

At least this was his formed impression once swore
His best to do in post some proof he reasoned
Of reach to bring endorsed place in the See's home
When not a bishop or a deacon or a lonelier

Man caring for those duteous souls who bred well!
Here he was not that but if it could be said
A lover for male feel of joins life-vital.

The irony could cause him smile to find that
His thoughts revolved to muse his self-coined title,
The Libertine Librarian of Vatican State!

117

HOW HE KEEPS A TITLE DESPITE HIS ABSENCE

The office gained in Vatican Library peer-robbed
Him of his time though less of mindful hope raised;
Obliged to spend eight to twelve hours in office,
He sat to wait on researchers while hours slipped . . .

His works went quoted in most towns of Europe,
Whose pains had not gained a substantial office;
So no provision grew for him in old age,
One cause of worry those times when he worried . . .

Twelve others took to work their work so he did;
Since these friends brought their news it was in gossip
Some hours slipped—irritating if he wished read.

The holidays he learned were long that closed five
Months down, so he learned to show up if needed,
And took that paid him to leave peers this job left!

118

1763:
HE IS MADE ANTIQUARIAN OF THE HOLY SEE

Appointed thence though library hours claimed him
To now-deceased Abbé Venuti's office,
The Superintendent of Antiquities was
To goal-use this role on seem made for trained him.

Time-ancient things could not come up to men than
He know of it so to direct their stood use.
Still spending himself for curation's proud cause,
He wished more sound provision for self-spent man!

Ah if he took the tonsure he could be sure
On mediation of his friends that met post
Would mean provision for his old age reached near!

Unwilling to breath-say the breviary caused
Him to vouch he born free was pains-taught if poor:
Since free would live free let him die free this most!

119

THE BOUDOIR ADVENTURER
GIACOMO CASANOVA VIEWS HIM IN NO COMPROMISING POSITION

The great lovemaker wrote I sought some few nights
The same room Winckelmann did just to show couth.
One time I saw slide out of a subdued youth
The scholar's proud limb who set breeches to rights!

Well *he* could not suppose I blushed to view this . . .
The youth quite quick to raise his breeches drew off,
To leave him searching for his words like choked up,
Soon finding some to use when used the voice his.

The best Greeks who most shone were homosexuals;
Greece none concealed it but our times demur here!
Slow to convict me of their stupid rituals,

I sought the light of practice in their error.
Casanova's Conviction: Unwilling to convict who learned from Greek selves,
He put to test whose theories groomed "researcher"!

120

TO CUT THE FIGURE
OF A MIDDLE-AGED GENTLEMAN IN INTRICATE PURSUIT OF PRIVILEGED YOUTHS

Such erudite man spoke his line while watched strain
Ease or increase some in the hearer's formed bounds:
His brother most beloved seemed to feel proud once
The compliments flowed but if he were touched then

A reflex seemed in place that showed too much time
Spent in conditioned circumstances' moored bounds.
The subject seemed to follow the mind-served founts
Of Grecian thinkers but did reached stroke brush him

He showed confused, grew alienated, sought space,
And then returned contrite till turned with great flight.
So much charge did two protons own in stood place

It ran through one its earthquake to unowned depths.
One was on pins to put deemed friend in eased head,
Stilled just through voicing of high-minded concepts!

121

YOUTHS CARELESS
OF HIS HOPE TO ENTER THE IDEAL ON THE STIMULUS OF MALE BEAUTY

You Peter, Nico, Friedrich got his letters,
Ones to unveil who told how his of men's wills
Seemed destined to revive the love between males,
So much too long held in that's slandered state worse!

You were the cultured young men most men's betters,
To witness how in Johann such work meant quest:
Love's form-ideal relationship no theme else
His private self went to give place with great force.

He meant to follow Plato's thought that said how
The contemplation of the beauty of youths
Discovers beauty of souls one's mind taught true!

You saw end short his high potential's sought use,
You who read less the sweeter books-deep shadow:
O such love younger men's selves still could not house!

122

WOULD HIS SO NOBLE FRIENDSHIPS BE OF LOVE?

His dedication of a work to Berg was
So worded that this caused to rise construction,–
On sense and beauty this work which betook men
To form their thoughts construing him on words' use!

His language was of love, found readers more cross.
Well love it was but mind let theirs most look on
The ideal rarified sort his words tokened,
Except which deemed him with the book Erotes'

Own Kallikratidas' mind Lucian's viewed love-window.
Some others rallied to defend him if then
Some others bolder owned his praise for things low . . .

Said of such love might be that Philip said when
The Thebans fell with wounds that just base tends who
Suspects corrupt of morals could possess them!

123

1762 TO 1764:
HELPFUL EXPRESSION AND AFFECTLESS PIVOT

Down own heart sank once Berg left Rome for Paris!
O 45 was old to need review love,
And old to weep for loss of unrenewed love,
And old to feel one wrenched for undeserved stress!

He tried to heal in words who sought the words best
To hold entombed own luminous-lined soul robbed!
He put in words the torments of pain's housed truth,
To will rich words though suffer that once nourished.

Too Mengs took note deciding he would offer
His own wife his friend lonelier . . . Margaret Mengs love
Like on the rebound? He wrote how the lover

Her health could use though just to chat he went up!
Spin, pun, jest, two tossed up to sink down proper,
I will end "virgin", "virtuous friendships" being loved!

124

HIS 1764 REPORT ON DISCOVERIES
OF HERCULANEUM AND SECOND SITE POMPEII UP TO OBSERVATIONS MORE

A guide to the king's cabinet his Letter,
He sought to guide who else obtained the king's nod;
The great guests on the Grand Tour writings lined up,
To read his sequel on the ancients' matter.

The site's discovered finds, book-ancient paper,
The scrolls' unrolling, the machine to bring that,
His Letter then Report up-lit works men met
In the collection like the Drunk Reclining Satyr.

Supposing Letter read his work Report on
Discoveries described the theater's structure–
The ancients' stagecraft and the stage performed on.

His Observations on the Architecture
Of Ancient Builders rendered Paestum stared on,
The Magna Graecia temples deemed men's treasure.

125

THE DEDICATEE
OF REPORT LOVE SUBSTITUTE JOHANN FUESSLI OF ZURICH AND POMPEIOMANIA

He stood in the same place companion-changed now.
His Letter roved with tourists while Report on
Discoveries he wrote to reach the scarfed one
Beside him J. H. Fuessli touched when thanked so.

Teemed finds were made appreciable if strange to
The wider public which his suns-high words bound
To see Pompeii for interest; this once more shown
Was to produce "Pompeiomania's" ranged plough.

The dawn of mass production was to be seed
To make unearthed finds of the ancient world spread
Till did pervade life. Dresses "à l'antique" made

A trend the mode . . . Urns "alla Pompeiana" married
The furniture to suit . . . "Pompeianized" breed
Of reproduction busts and paintings served pride.

126

PHENOMENA
AS DESCRIBED IN THE HISTORY OF ART IN ANTIQUITY,
AN IMMEDIATE CLASSIC TO EARN HIM THE TITLE FATHER OF METHOD IN ART HISTORY

To want a chronological historian-
Scribed record of all antique art whose grand plan
Wove in the trends of ancient art and ancient
Life to reveal the process which both worlds blent.

His masterpiece The History of Art in
Antiquity won literature standing,
To show in art organic growth, peak, then end-
Decline in match of civilization's marching.

A glowing world of insight, climate, freedom,
To heighten social, mental, soulful shapes in,
Did lie behind the great works to call Grecian . . .

A politics still under ideas pliant,
A noble will that sought shaped forms' enrichment
Achieved the goal of art pure beauty's statement!

127

WINCKELMANN REPEATS HIS INJUNCTION
TO ARTISTS HE FIRST ENJOINED IN THOUGHTS ON THE IMITATION OF GREEK WORKS

The true-souled artist chooses forms from nature,
Ones to support his scheme of art-refined shapes.
His soul refines them that in their combined traits
The whole is formed in beautiful-formed measure.

A moderation makes each choice tends each sure
To reach the goal of beauty's plan sublime-faced,
Obtained once scheme subordinates to fine taste
The ugly, stray, characteristic feature.

Subordinating idiotic things leaves
The ideal beauty's shape to space-dwell put-best
Sublime intents the true-souled artist's sense feels.

It leaves refinement on one's vision brought thus
To the harmonious, proportionate states man wills
On over the depressed waste doomed for bodies.

128

THE POET
ON WINCKELMANN'S MOST OUTSTANDING AESTHETIC OBSERVATION

One's estimation of thing beauty called taste,
His own he showed was owed high-minded concepts.
His love of men involved the sense which found life's
More general form was free from womb or breast use.

He wrote those who observe thing beauty just based
On women though observe none when it own-dwells,
So seem moved less or seem unmoved to fondness
Once lent the chance to view the beauty holds males,

Will seldom own the instinct for art's termed bounds,
Or house sense for the full range that forms art great,
Or find excitement from the art Greece formed once.

Supreme in Grecian motive is the male-to-bear trait,
And seeing beauty just in women's charged zones
One lacks the talent's use that serves great art's need.

129

THE TROPHY HE PEDESTALS AS FAILS HIMSELF

His own achievement spawns the great man's crisis.
Ah what can follow one's achievement shown deep?
Another one demands some charge off found sleep,
Some re-won outlook, or some take owed self-rest.

His writing purpose took his straightened strictness,
Ah too long shown for strength to drain his own life!
He put his time but health too in work's bound heap,
And free if finished just his wracked health he faced.

The time spent courting beauteous of boy eunuchs,
Spent pouring on each line of face indifferent
So went to write the beauteous wording uncrushed,

He owned was void, left not von Berg if left him!
Ah wretch how long in need when writing punished,
The nearest outcome one's thinned body lived in!

130

1765:
THE ACCOUNTING ON IT SHOWN A FINE DISDAIN

Was he who showed dependent on him more robbed?
To be read in sold books though bound to think poor
Himself owed what? A friend born just gold-miner?
Two sets of books did one keep numbers queer proof

Of how his writings though sold throughout Europe
Were short of bid power than to keep him scant there?
In grand life too grand would he too much spend near
Such heir of managers of gold swept worlds off?

Accounts of their self-serving postures put down,
So what? The Abbé Ruggieri till now deemed sweet,–
A friend just shot himself who seemed in talk sound!

One suffered moment's sadness too could bring that
To him midst of this sumptuous brilliance looked on,
An ingrate who should quit these clouds or end dead.

131

AN ABBÉ RUGGIERI DEAD AND A SAXON POST SO

Ah Ruggieri who just shot himself when
Owed friendship's feel on both sides better than that!
An exuberant talker though still confidant held
In sweet trust for the words he weighed if best reined

Was no more meaning no more strength to his friend.
Albani too was turning old what meant that
He Johann should think of his future when what?
His heart saw Saxony the place to bide in,

Since the Elector Frederick Augustus II was
One reason he was in Rome did his searched thought
Serve to remember the nice pension's just cause.

The prince long said to wish him make his court proud
A Superintendent of Museum's post used—
Yet peace with Prussia bound rich spending more cut!

132

A PRUSSIAN POST EXTENDED UP TO RETRACTED

Moved-force King Frederick chance-imagined him in
The place of Gautier la Croze himself deceased thus
His Superintendent of the Library post
One to give Johann would its terms stand mentioned.

Assistant Nicolai brought close that post's extension,
As deputized under Colonel Icilius
Wrote he should seek to be paid if propitious
One thousand to two thousand thalers when went!

Two thousand he demanded though his king cooled.
So he replied ten years' experience in Rome earns
More than the same years' number just spent in cold

Use calculating increments for dumb forms
Like parabolic lines, curves, shapes that mean what!
Saint Petersburg's own Maupertuis' used own terms.

133

1765:
HOW HE BEGS A POST FROM POPE CLEMENT XIII

An old roué once said that that too dumb to be said
Is sung which might deter each man of mind willed!
So Johann better to provide for himself
Sought the Rotunda's post no choir could tell filled.

Adieu Monsieur Abbé with hand in book but *he* said
To one who researched on the porch to find wealth
In Nonnius' Dionysiacus then failed
That genuflection which the pope should see made!

His majordomo said the book he reads is
One pagan no doubt . . . His patron who took that up
Said more than so . . . He once declined to say mass,

So let the post of Bocca della Verità drop.
Stay he said to the majordomo it was
The choir I shirked mine that Rotunda's, great pope!

134

D'HANCARVILLE:
THE WRITER, ART THEORIST, AND AMATEUR ART DEALER

Pierre-François Hugues fixed for him the title
Of Baron d'Hancarville on taste's pretensions.
The heir of one insolvent he showed keen sense
To move in the best circles which those rich filled . . .

He got the French Ambassador's help which let
Him do Berlin so clasped in his the king's hands.
He got imprisoned draughting false bills when clenched
To write there his excuse of Politics Willed . . .

One Württemberg prince paid his debts whose service
He entered charged to take the Corsican-teemed
Isle with the Princess of Brazil—which failing turned his

Sight to Ambassador Hamilton pimped.
His sought wealth helped him broker such art purchase
As brought Antiquities from the Cabinet print . . .

135

THE BARON PUBLISHES ANTIQUITIES
OUT OF THE COLLECTION OF THE HONORABLE WILLIAM HAMILTON ILLUSTRATED BY
THE VIRTUOUS FRANCESCO MORELLI

The meeting he formed let the Porcinaris
And Hamilton meet so in walking those two
Toured their collection theirs just then the whole slew
Of vases from the past unearthed in parts which

Included Herculaneum. To wish this art pleased
His *own* once this was bought how else could both do?
The dealer wrote descriptions then involved who
Made rich prints of the painted scenes of theirs each.

Antiquities of Hamilton when printed
In four books proved one of the best productions,
And grew his profit great . . . The sequel blended

His ideas on art as developed through means
Owed to techniques, aesthetics, and precedents that
Were joined to cultural and religious notions.

136

MORE OF D'HANCARVILLE'S MOTIONS

Again high living drew him down from debt's weight.
He got free of his creditors in Naples
Once stepped in the Grand Duke of Tuscan peoples,
To grant protection so this let him be paid

To oversee the copper-plate prints each made
To show entire the Medici in sables.
His second fortune might have bloomed to have this
Work wrought but he could not elude his fixed need

Or hold fast to his luck so got on wrong side
Again of someone high . . . Homecoming found him
In just the place he left, here just rebounded

To host his correspondent Johann come round
To think he might dare venture some on ground that
Outspoken words lent slip's chance to risk one prone.

137

ACQUAINTANCE JOHANN VON RIEDESEL,
D'HANCARVILLE SEEN FIT TO BE HIS HELP

A duel might be fought on words Alcubierre
Encountered to describe him in the writings
On Herculaneum both in mind of each since . . . ,
One still determined to be sound than sorry.

Years on the chance existed that he there be
Accompanied thus take the risk of meetings:
The model-liberated John Wilkes said things
Implied to mean in Naples risked could tarry.

Such plan evaporated to let old loom
Of fear regrow to join considerations
On how the sites' doors seemed shut to him.

But now he got rid of his past evasions:
He called on Riedesel friend once to hope in,
He called on d'Hancarville to boost relations.

138

HIS 1767 DINNER WITH LUIGI VANVITELLI,
AND COME TO UNWIND JUST WHEN SOMETHING ERUPTS

One in Caserta should tend dined with *none* else:
One joined the royal architect when dined there!
The two were nearing midnight when shown timelier
Vesuvius erupted house-boards bound stressed!

A fine black gravel dropped on the wild country's
Scene green below the sooty veil's descent rarer.
Soon reconnected principals proud friends three,
Men feeling vigor life when healthier-found feels . . . ,

Johann, Herr Riedesel, Monsieur d'Hancarville those.
To look on each sprung from his rest in matter,
The three know that their spirits wish the hike posed.

A plan is formed to reach the mount-high crater.
Eruption Monday Wednesday loomed for this cause:
A guide would need to be hired just to get there!

139

THE ASCENT

Eruption Monday Wednesday seemed the right day
To start the toil-wrenched climb of Mount Vesuvius.
A guide, the three men, three of servants rose thus
On one side of the mount near evening's great play.

Outset with torches these were lit with light's sway
On the soon-darkened path which formed a hot crust.
To see the mouth the group was forced to use just
A part of burning stream which caused the guide say

To them too difficult . . . ! Those three intent sought
His change of mind on words then used sticks on him
To beat him till complied! On went the man taught,

To lead them past the ancient- to the new-brimmed.
He drifted back though d'Hancarville pushed on hot—
Willed Johann, Riedesel like-heartened through him.

140

EPIPHANY

As leather of the shoes cracked so the soles scorched
To keep the men on dance feet up to reached mouth,
The three passed to the rim to feel quite pleased but
To find for soot it nil to peer things though searched!

Here in the smell of sulfur with their mouths parched,
The men stripped nude though if to be to each couth
Stood in but shoes dressed in the muscles each loved
To set their doves down on the steam of rocks harsh!

How near the rim brought moved Empedocles' jump,
Out of the shed clothes rocks-dried the perspired wet,
The group exuded to feel strength which helps some!

Once did eat on stood soles, once winged of birds bid
To exit them within the mouth mixed streams swum,
A show of lust there seemed survived when more set!

141

THE DESCENT

At midnight these nude men took their return quest,
And down through perils did not put their clothes on
Till viewed the first stir of the crowd of those wound
On their displaced condition's stream of earned rest!

So in their breeches just drawn up these burned next
To whisk drinks from their carriages void motion . . . ,
And there these drank to quench the thirst exposing
The tread went over smoking rock some hours each!

So too was seen one great fact how such hot stream
Did not one deemed-fortuitous boulder serve sound
To stop it so divert it to a low bend

The vale of which was filled high up to earth's crown,
Portici even its museum would end
Beneath that lava palace-high whose force doomed!

142

WINCKELMANN'S TRIUMPH
IN SEEDING THE NEO-CLASSICAL TENDENCIES OF MEN IN ALL THE COUNTRIES OF EUROPE (I)

One best of art's sublime souls who attempted
To match the spirit as well as the forms found
Admired in time's present when unearthed one
Of ancient Greece or Rome was Mengs this Mengs said

To be the man formed art as Johann dreamed it.
His contribution Europe's different courts owned;
His studio housed groups of men of art shone;
His role David soon was to match who when met

Mengs was to learn of Johann's soul-lit theories.
His studio powered revolution through art
High-souled, technique-strong, lustre-brilliant, work-rich.

Imitation? Robert Adam leading Scots arch-
Itect built new Greek temples . . . Out of "Etrurias"
The trade in Greek-frieze reproductions flowered.

143

WINCKELMANN'S TRIUMPH
IN SEEDING THE NEO-CLASSICAL TENDENCIES OF MEN IN ALL THE COUNTRIES OF EUROPE (II)

World's soul-transporting grand chord of the Altes
Museum or the Konzerthaus Karl Schinkel
Struck be for mind-pure heights-sought grand feel.
The imitation when outwent that owed his

Word imitate but who great then makes great each
Who does with strong perception of the end willed.
His moving sculptures beauteous with things' swell
Antonio Canova shaped for sought heights.

Traits, content, contours, method, skills perfected
Were to subordinate to the demands of beauty.
Description of the Incised Gems Collected

By Baron Stosch their reading how shone should be
The forger Calandrelli undetected
Or minute-painting Smart, Crosse, Richard Cosway.

144

1768:
A SORT OF HOMECOMING

Years up to thirteen since famed Johann saw home,
Time's wish seemed to return such native honored!
A sculpture-restoring friend to help him homeward,
Bartolomeo Cavaceppi was to draw on.

The sight of Tyrol served to panic Johann.
Was it the mountains served up guilt that sundered?
The rushed-in German guilt to tense one son's heart
He sensed off peasants of contempt for love's fount.

Bart saw him look in nervous breakdown's breaking
But talked sense into him that up to Munich
The two went when near Ratisbon his racked friend

Turned back to stop in choice Vienna once reached.
Bart traveled to Berlin where Frederick shaken
Told him Johann was dead of murder's shown strike.

145

1768:
A SORT OF LEAVETAKING

All Europe's march to ideal beauty owed him—
Aestheticized of male desire's life champion!
He was owed honor though the high-held same man
Was fifty when things left were feared revoked then!

It now was long since he said Greek art showed men
Humanity's most high-in-climb achievement—
To owe the simple nobleness its great theme
And calm grandeur its tone of thought-imbued time.

He now seemed on the precipice between worlds
And breathed with vertigo from the cooled back-drop
To void the sun-drenched Italy which men nursed.

He needed back though needed new to take love:
Own swash return imposed the vow for things first
His in the past he should not lose if reached prop!

146

HE DECLINES
PRINCE KAUNITZ'S OFFER OF A SITUATION ADVANTAGEOUS TO HIM

Acquiring worlds honed thoughtful connoisseurship.
He could help build the fantast which did house him,
In Cardinal Albani's brand of view-high wrought-fine
Aesthetic choices made rooms male for power's self.

So not in rococo midst formed of theirself
Did he seem free to take the offer brought him,
Once heard this with the honors there bestowed on
The great taste-maker of his times seen more male.

So he declined their help in curlish Schönbrunn
Advancing him for some post it was thought strange
He could refuse though code could not presume him

So lived or so ensconced this served to moot change.
The arbiter of art inside a home lum-
Inous through great will he stuck with his true stance.

147

ARRIVAL
AND INSPECTION OF THE PORT'S WATERFRONT

Such one remained a short time in their great Wien,
Time limited to just the ceremonies
Prince Kaunitz shared with her his mother Empress
Maria Theresa who took to meeting

One gold medallion just the prince would give him,
And one gold though two silver which the empress
Would give him for that compliment profoundness
Achieved to earn so moved the world received him.

On leaving them he traveled in a post coach
And drew up Wednesday June 1 just at twelve noon,
In front of the Osteria Grande viewed close.

But steps down spared he willed the carriage still on,
And went to port near the hotel to talk thus
On some one's of the docked ships he should sail on.

148

ENDORSEMENT OF A SITE ON THE OPEN STREET

One is thrown to the wind when in the crowd's churn,
And just shared motive much dissolves the self's one;
Were this not present distance would show reasoned,
More his who reasoned over else who most swarmed.

A sight of buns passed if from this his thought turned
To owe chance to endorse a thing which pleased him,
And this which drew up reached was one piss station . . . ,
And hours spent sole would bust him out for no scorn.

He thought the piss was in him there to stream forth,
So stopped the carriage to dismount then stroll down,
To own through him those public duties men stored!

He freed his means to do such when sensed how one
Was watching him like he so seemed did when stared,
To watch one stepped up free his member how hung.

149

SILK IN TRIESTE

Swirled town Trieste the maritime Silk Road's end!
The whiff of port was brought him with time's one pissed
And raised its stream of more than his of bounced whiffs,
The smell of common mix none new to Rome's him.

A pissoir too in town Trieste brought some's blend,
On force owed mixed-up bustle moved their bound needs,
As in contingent needs of men's half-shown selves:
Out in the one piss station some man watched him.

He turned to this man sight to scope his freed limb:
His main limb seemed to drop bound weight to own new
The meaning for the simple-nobleness theme!

Its hung poise showed the calm grandeur of one so
Sublime it seemed to cause what wise smile reached him,
On owner's face of him who stood in bound know!

150

TRICK IN SERVICE

A motion no a quick tic of the head caused
The man to step up with him in the carriage.
The door was shut when it sealed up their marriage,
Veiled in the carriage while it turned for streets passed.

The strangers did not touch, to touch quite needless
In two men panting for how showed to dare such.
The silence saw them each on each to stare flushed,
To search some portent in the mood of great stress!

Want to experience it? So tense seemed being,
It caused him Johann to react with great twitch . . .
His feet flew while his knees knocked while his hands went

In two directions like to end on sight stretched.
He recomposed his twisted form when then seemed
To speak in calm of plans his quickened self hatched.

151

THE MAIN SQUARE OF TOWN'S PROXIMAL HOTEL

The carriage stopped at the Osteria Grande,
The town's superb hotel. You here will live I
Deem well . . . ! I do live here deemed well if I be!
His name? Francesco. Winckelmann's . . . ? Giovanni.

He brought him home? Yes. What room would this man's be?
Here Johann saw him pause. You soon will tell me:
I live in different travelers' rooms said felt sigh . . .
He found most off the port's ships once was seen *he*,

Francesco—or his main limb—thing for men's woo!
Want to hand-stroke it? He got in line when did saw
His suitor nerve-racked, menaced, sweat-moist, glimpse-new.

He took his time-lent place in this man's set raw:
Pygmalion saw the life crude's gifted pimped true,—
Yet if reached up so to teach culture held straw!

152

HE SETS THE TWO OF THEM UP IN THE WORLD

Francesco might live in male travelers' rooms but
Here Johann wished more civilized arrangements!
The concierge could let two rooms each entrance-
Opposed in mirror doors hall so went down stood.

The men soon settled in the rooms if one's would
Be the more furnished with his travel-seen things.
One's wait on the right ship to sail two's evenings
Took up with dinners then things set up on mood.

What was the basis for this hook-up went wrong?
One shook off Puritan thing Pietism
The second time in life for lived hour sense-strong.

So on revisit did scenes of the past swim
In present mind of one who found this friend hung
And willing to burn up bored wait with teased him.

153

THE TWO DROP INTO DINNER IN A DINING ROOM

It just was chance then-destined them in some mix!
Air round noon stirred in service of the main meal.
Once seated Johann spoke of his then-planned sail:
I need to take a ship to Rome if one is

To sail so wonder is some word to be heard on this?
Francesco knew of no ship schedules himself
But owned he did since wished to seem to him help.
He spoke impromptu of some names seen on ships,

Or heard in port when passing men discussed them.
The ship of Captain Ragusini will sail
He said on whim this begged to show his view then.

Yes sure once dinner here is done will I tell
You how to spot it just midst of the room lent!
Seen one stood begged to lead them to that vessel.

154

HOW HE IS SATISFIED
ON HIS LEAVING TRIESTE WITHIN ONE WEEK

In port the bustle rose up just when need bound.
The gruff man Ragusini moved sole through lull.
Her cargo was not on ship least since caused sail
He said how know such lading's time to be done.

Another captain one Vittorio's ship one week on
Would sail to reached Ancona's port without fail.
He would just need that's lading to end so sailed
On Saturday or Sunday . . . Such to make sound,

Two ducats more than was the passage-money
Was promised in gratuity for his word.
The ship would not complete her lading Sunday;

On Monday following that Johann reached forth
To take as guaranty and earnest-money
A sum to mean on Tuesday he would leave port!

155

A WEEK TO START A MONTH MIDDLE OF WEEK

Still on look this was Wednesday first this great date
To find him in the pair stepped in one pleased mood,
As things brought to one's liking went to ease both
And bring the street up under stride in feel great.

On walking from the port to rooms that waited,
A coffee-house both entered which would be brought
To feature for the place their week would see both
To meet, drink, or eat if not in the hotel did.

On finishing their cups both strolled the street up
To their hotel then stepped up to opposed rooms.
Here Johann faced his friend though failed to lead love

To blossom bursting forth in one of those rooms.
He seemed to grow amnesia for things met both,
And thanked him for his help like it were just nonce.

156

LOVE IN A MAN'S DEFINITION LIT BETWEEN THEM

One beat paused in expressed appreciation–
To look his friend in face while praised help in words
Up to when contact loss let speech fail in force–
He moved to stress his point with his upraised hand.

He was on point of touching the man's breast grand:
Will then revolved the hand just backs of fingers
To rest so on his breast just knuckle-lengths pressed
On shirt of him the curved flesh caused to be fanned.

The gesture one too diffident caused this friend
To grip it with a great grip which compressed that
And pushed it firm on his breast with his great hand!

Surprised the shier's other hand when raised met
His gritting friend's now-second grip swept this man
In room of his who went down with down-thrust head.

157

A FIRST NIGHT'S SUPPER IN ARCANGELI'S ROOM

One's prospect of ship's sail remained for view since
The older's if not idol's room-view looked down
On the hotel-side inner port both walked down,
On the great dock Mandrachio long in bows' lengths.

In room were conquered unruled worries those times
He found reposed or rallied friendship brooked them . . . :
The ship bound for Ancona seemed just docked long
In lie on water though served for wrought comments.

The night of Wednesday first his friend went in stroll
Amidst the bustle though on his return sent
A coffee like he drank to him let his cool.

Yet once the lights were brought his visit turned them
To light chat till the servants brought a meal rolled
In on a cart between them which helped share them!

158

SENSUOUS INTELLIGENCE (I)

Who seemed the worldlier was something soon told,
Although it switched both seen new on the moment.
Soon Johann if took that role unbecoming
The older man redeemed this with each bound stroll.

In talks he blended currents though now unschooled
Seemed his one reader for each rolling-round theme.
Aesthetic theory, time, taste, sculpture bound them
To note the boundless sides of men one found whole.

To talk or hear of Socrates, sublime Greeks,
The pure forms, the ideal zone, the implied real,
The Spartan youths who practiced naked witnessed

His categories . . . Help this caused one's pleased self
Went conduit-like his ego to his penis
In monolithic loop bored from such preached wealth.

159

SENSUOUS INTELLIGENCE (II)

One erudite point might tend that which woke him—
To weigh the sense that housed contending beauties
So cause him best stand mode-transposed of bodies—
The lunk, the dolt, the ego this hung bloke seemed!

One mentor might theme-use the worship tokened—
To suck this bloke this idol for men's wrought nights—
Although he Johann *soon* sensed how to hole-switch
The more-drunk idol that the limb whose bulk went

Sprung out of mouth then worked force in his rectum,
To cause thing burdensome to wing in choice space,
A somber, well-imposed, smooth-whole delight then!

Still views of form this nude-posed idol's took watch
To grow breaths tense-deep for his volume-fixed bum,
Inside of which to wish for thrust when should much.

160

A SCHEDULE BOUND TO SCHEDULE-BOUND SHIP

The two friends settled into scheduled things stoked
It seemed to form some customs round stood limbo.
Each morning from this time forth both self-went so
To take their breakfast less observed of men looked.

Once left the breakfast coffee-house the friends took
A walk back to the great hotel though went through
At different times so none supposed them into
Each other's selves like feeling men once seem mock.

Once or twice more both met there during up's hours,
And in like manner found themselves at noon meals
Of the hotel, reposed, or braced for evening outdoors

To take their walks on each's side which showed nice.
The third day since companionship took such course
His friend turned up the heat to question one pressed . . .

161

MOTIVE
IN LIE BENEATH MOTIVE IN LIE BENEATH MOTIVE

Each state owes people's militarized selves' strength,
The thing that over-reaches bounds so speaks men's
Speech to their peers held in contempt of each since,
Mere weaklings to the ordered might that seals rank.

A state thus men's excuse to find them each strange,
Sized like removed from recognition's slipped means,
The excess of the peopling's thus unrecognized ends
Is state's excuse to treat them brusque with its range.

So no time humanized dehumanized lives
Each soul beneath their bundled power invests State!
Speech turns collective-willed so speaks to each else,

You now will serve to please us owed our reach great,
You now will serve our each demand with said reach,
You to submit, surveil, impose on, hold in check right.

162

ENDLESS VENTRILOQUISM OF THE DUMMY STATE

Since militarized selves must birth each reached state,
Each helpless one but knows the world from conquest.
Although must *seem* omniscient for men's homeplace,
Each nothing knows of men's selves or men's real fate.

So it wills souls formed on the forced speech fails that,
And the intrusive need's obtrusion men deem one just
To ease their sort's will over-reached on doomed dust.
Ventriloquist men come to prompt state's speech said

To each themselves unknown to it too growth-spread,
Who tempt to pass their masks between them in front
Of blind collective power . . . ! Said since we now need,

You caught, to verify you . . . ! Our proof of men bound
Your burden you must hold our proof to show that
You are that one you say you are of stream's doomed!

163

HE IN FEEL OF MOTIVE
IN LIE BENEATH MOTIVE IN LIE BENEATH MOTIVE

The cook might choose in innocence some first chore
To lead him to his strange skill helping propped men!
Yet once the corpse lies bloodied do the spouse then
The cook seem willed not too removed from murder!

So might the hero of the pleasure surer
Seem suspect till of this itself he shows meant
To own some crime for so long feeding slopped men!
So might the farmer who feeds beasts hold their care

His right to slaughter those detained to feed crushed.
Yet farmers in collection boost their honor,
To leave sole homicides bruised from each life voiced.

The hero hung Francesco suffered rumor,
Yet just a thief of thing not life found each choice
Of his forced on the branding saw him doomed more.

164

HOW JUST JESUS OF NAZARETH
TURNED STATE VENTRILOQUISM BACK ON ITSELF

Our need that need of men through tending each one
Upswept into the state we then tell ones mirrored
You must show us our wish of proof for own word.
Once Jesus asked such state who do you say that I am . . .

Sized bounds grown out of "courteous" recognition,
State's sole excuse men's excess peopling conquered
To be unrecognized, state's caused will wants spared
Souls to show proof whose reach "identified" them!

Your burden is to furnish us our proof that
You are that one you say you are of growth's men:
The state thus is to let men treat men brusque-willed.

But not without repeating Jesus could one–
One like Arcangeli–change bounds that owed State!
A change denied him his willed self was stop-bound!

165

THE FIRST DARE:
FRANCESCO DARES GIOVANNI TO TELL HIS FAMILY NAME

The third day brood-dark trick said neither knows his
Seen friend by family name though knows his balls or
His rectum loved between buns men must call queer,
Whose worship was when stood low parts in up-ness.

We seem just John and Francis said friend cold-wise,
Although this seemed through warmth's Italian color
The custom for that south both proved to hold dear,
And these facts this friend noted with some process!

Youth went first . . . The fourth day Arcangeli leaned
To say his family's name to him paused frozen.
Out with it said tense friend now surname be named!

Francesco: You must hear that our host suspects you who seem
Some rogue to his high guests? Say then do say then
Mock-put Signor John John your family's true name!

166

HOW IN ACQUIESCENCE HE CONFIDES HIS NAME

His spite grew with incensed spike of fierce feelings,
Although to be done with such scene's emboldened
Young man he quite relented that he told him
He was a man with no suspicious dealings.

He was not so opposed when scorned to tell things.
His name was Johann Winckelmann he told him,
Then other things he put out in the open.
He would show him his passport-same medallions,

And letters naming him to banking houses
Like Lucchesi in Görz or Tomazzi in Venice,
And things else so in nature to produce his

Impression more correct which was his friend's wish.
To be gripped on his shirt's carnelian bosses,
He said so much till ungripped with two hands' fists!

167

THE SECOND DARE:
FRANCESCO DARES GIOVANNI TO SHOW HIS MEDALS

So on June fourth the young man won his said name.
One day on his trick wondered on things mentioned,
In walking mentioned medals which most leaned-on
The young man took his promise he could see them!

On Sunday first June fifth he showed them his friend
Ere both wound in the hotel's mid-day meal's scene.
His stepped-out friend described these to the same man
Who ran the coffee-house his soleness sat in.

Here or then in a secret tavern chosen—
But unrevealed so this supplied him thought's space—
He wove a dream that were their love in both shown,

Were this John willing to own theirs for those guests—
His own love ever evident in how hung—
Then he would take up life with him in Rome's breast.

168

DOOR TAG

A door opposed to other door is opened:
The face of one shows piqued to wait with tense poise.
The other door is checked then his door stands closed:
The face of one the other shows his closed then.

A time no face is seen when step out both men,
So face meets face demure for how shared one blush:
Each one frets due such catch of view since tends used
And needs to stand impression-fixed for love's stand!

A lot of time is spent in common eating,
Discussing, sharing, teaching, walking through streets;
But Johann needs time resting from unbright mind

And re-reads Lucian's works droll interest brought his.
He dares not let the sex-drowsed bloke sleep with him;
Sent off for room-sleep one must else keep up checks!

169

SECRET STEPPINGS-OUT OF ONE

So went the two this week to tend men's needs met.
Time spent in secret plead of shot sperm helped men
To bide the void wrought sore the parting-willed one.
The lies both selves told served to keep men's secret

And helped selves stand sure on relationship's need,
When these were shown attempting just to brighten
One's wait . . . So feigned forms tended heightened,
Seen when affirming the sly-altered adage that said—

To change two vowels—that said the subset buggers
Must not be choosers . . . How think either was such,
Though both remembered when took better lovers!

Too both supposed ones "nicer" neared—be so much
Unseen for Johann—though Francesco brought doors
To open some those wee hours Johann just dozed.

170

THE SELF AS THE BENCH:
THE TRUE-MALE SEX DIAGNOSIS OF ARCANGELI

The bloke his friend was not his friend once left him;
The bloke one idol-proud owed means of self-bench,
The form of *power's* bench individual life tends
Once self-invents control's sense like own-destined!

The weight of his main limb formed him exception;
The rules must bend since grander is his self-sense!
His depth is just self-interest though it feels ranged
With plumb of limb owed worship for its grand line!

He sees this much though blind to peer-lent beauty
His soul is owed group code thus needs respect-sex
To bring for his hers opposite of wrought "I".

Once saw that his limb—wanton—could submit each,
He grew to need the fix that for some brought fee
Saw him subdue men like girls the "true male" seeks.

171

ROTATING DOORS IN THE TOWN TRIESTE

On night he let his pride prowl through the brothels:
Here too his self-bench domineered like did power's.
His drove the coin-mint both directions spite-forced
On men for paid fee when his bench subdued males,

Although lent girls' or women's still-subdued selves,
The fee he took not—lovelier—paid them each theirs!
Atoned for trespass he restored through self-source
Of womb whose virtue cleansed him of so-rude else.

He was the idol of the men though then was
The savior of the women whose own trespass
Was saved through contact with one grander penis . . . !

So robbing men he paid the girls whose sex was
Wet-nurse of his own mind their occupied nest,
Although on straight end his set pride was each male's.

172

DRUNK

Up with his thoughts on Lucian when he woke then
In wee hours, Johann was to hear how night's quiet
Was turned to sound of steps went up in steps right
Beside his door then stopped with discord tokened.

The sound of clinking metal then most struck him!
The door thought opened near stood opposite side,
To mean up to own door Francesco tripped tight,
And since was drinking *more* required one's look in,

To tell the state deemed just returned from night-life.
Out of his door shot Johann's head then person.
Suspected sooner when did sound drunk each step,

The tripping-drunk friend uplit Johann's pert mind:
The chance was now to turn him in his straight trip,
And head him right to Johann's room of queer theme!

173

DESIRE

The great kind man he was took care for this friend:
He walked tight him so propped so steadied his steps,
And paused to lower him down on luscious silk sheets,
His whole concern the strike on puff of head's length.

Mengs' pictures of the angels went through his mind:
He sensed off of one else his touch-fond sweet reach.
His friend he undressed; to wipe off his sweat wished,
A towel he took; the brow he dried wet beads ringed.

But not proceeding to his friend's main limb stroked,
The stroke-lengths he diffused to bring parts starven;
And not proceeding to his friend's main limb sucked,

The suck-points he diffused to bring so-served them;
The scrotum, rectum, thigh-pits swirled of limp bloke,
Who of himself raised up for more his rectum.

174

SLIP-SLICK

He Johann's luck was holding for on quick check
His friend he found was emptied out like just dumped:
One deeper mission of two fingers' use found
The mucous lining so clean it was slip-slick.

So this would be a miracle of wished sex,
To use the force of the deprived sense caused one:
The womb's long-stood role would bid impetus-bound
Him to delight in centered plumb of cheek-cheek!

The versatile self was returned in true form:
He went on wing on foremost wing through deep space
And relished from reverse his conqueror now turned.

His mind was the whole seat of this tensed rite's praise,
And in the moment destined his to shoot sperm,
His friend's shot firmed the lining like forced ribs raised.

175

SPLIT SELF

The drunk one entered trust in Johann's eased mind,
Who took heart so the first time let trick him sleep.
He slept this night in Johann's room when then deep
Own sleep let sober sleep like drunk beside friend.

Appeased he slept so well that he quite missed him
Once woke up sole in bed. When did his friend leave?
He failed to see the dark turn in the time left
Him to weigh sole the shared event for night's men.

The room just walls saw him up first wake sober,
And on self's sense of split identity frown,
And in one stroke of turned seat swipe up blood there,

And hot with strike look down on who prone slept on.
Trick tasted his own period in blood's mirror
Of who he was become on seeming self-ruin!

176

AMBIT

The hot Francesco dressed with ire then stormed out
And vented in town streets his length-long hot stride.
He was incensed to feel the rage the bloke might
Who feels transposed on no will but was scorn owed.

He went toward the place near brothels wormed but
He found the girls since when long up were now slept.
He went toward the country though found no sweet,
The girls on chore or round like ones that earned trod.

He walked back to the town-walls no less stirred up,
And in a morning's tavern sought force not drink,
And there where people flirted sewed his world up.

He there decided he would not show one thing,
No sign of thing off but feign peace while worked up
A plan not Jesus brought to tempt so wrought mind!

177

TOKEN

His friend missed caused the one then sole to wish in
A friendship token which remembrance held stirred!
He seized on the first concept long-crossed field art
Would raise in his mind this to draw such-sized thing

Or do a rubbing like intaglios lived in.
The two met on the street whereon their steps paired.
Behind his feign of feeling peace one gathered
More information on the night which split him.

The two stepped in a shop where Johann purchased
A pencil, paper, penknife, tools frottage used;
Francesco dwelt on knives he saw with stare glazed.

The two cut to the pastry and fromage shops,
Then to the Osteria Grande place brought their stash,
Although the planned frottage to wait on speech use.

178

SET UP NOT TO BACK DOWN

Dismissed, rest shared none, Arcangeli walked from
The stood streets to the stationer's shop sold knives.
He paid the cost, transacting such through two lives,
So with one witness sensed he could not back down.

The scruff was going to get it were words stalked one;
He heard this told the scruff's self be this now thief's.
He heard on switch its cause-words said of two selves,
Heard I am going to kill him when then fact seemed!

Such whispered on the street with life breathed in it . . . ,
Ear heard close the remote bound to occur soon.
The turner of him must die, witness of what one did!

On points he tried to save ruin of the sore-swooned,
Split-double life took the received news shown dread
That who he took to screw screwed *him* to curse on.

179

SURVEIL OF THE CLOTH

Out on built streets he sensed his rectum's loose feel.
Once sensing how for trim buns hot sun swept down
A street-long path to be stopped on his stride's pump . . . ,
He stopped himself up near a windowed shop's wall.

He rotated his breeches-in buns pose-willed,
Turned self to see if orbs-rolled cloth were spilled on;
The thought to feel form in this street to stride down
Was that he stood his rectum's blood on cloth spilled . . .

The sun-touched butt-stretched cloth the window showed was
Still spotless no trace in the centermost seam
Of that loose feel up in between his buttocks.

He clinched them each face to remind him of the crowd's mind,
And stepped inside a dry-goods shop that sold ropes,
And bought a rope to garrote the man screwed him!

180

VAMPIRE HARPIES

He went that evening to the brothels' grouped girls,
Went soonest seeking to redeem transposed being.
He wished them to re-sex him male who used them
To reach back to own wholeness of male-true force.

His sex-reversed self-death went on in mood worse
The thoughts to burst in sundering his whole being.
He saw girls when then felt one when then saw him
A girl who let his John inside his hole cursed.

He sought to use his strength this night of romping,
Though each ensemble of the girls showed him girl,
A girl who grimaced in contempt of humped him.

He screwed the girls without restoring time's world
To undo sense of his reversed sex bound slumped,
To feel the lint stuffed in him own blood since hard!

181

RUBBLE HEAPS

The screwed male should hear pivot or expand mind,
But no words entered this one's mind could use help.
The best word versatile worlds from his drooped self,
He fell down through mind—restoration's time spent,

To win no former ease to spare male-wrenched bind!
His rest would not near; he-girl's witness moved still;
And he being she his soul's wound O would not heal!
(One must die—secret die with him—to redeem time.)

How was the earthquake taking place the strange in,
As if self-crumbling to remove saw streets cracked
And buildings sunk in rocks which left deranged him!

He walks while whispers I am going to kill him,
Though hears how the stalked scruff is going to get it,
Who screams from rubble I am going to kill him . . .

182

ALL SEEMING WELL

The Frisson Dies Out: He reached the Osteria Grande of their dwelt norm
A bit self-bitten, wind-blown, though not crumbled.
He even saw in state of one sex-humbled
To wait on his John's killing not to feel churned . . .

Besides he wished to show strength ever self-sworn.
Such was to give chance healing to his stumped self,
To own it did him no worse though was humped till
His shot streaked to affirm the change in swell form.

The Frottage Takes Life: The time come he put down on wood his main limb
And saw it pencil-traced then graphite-rubbed on
The paper to record that's strength still undimmed!

He punished his friend/traitor when now mounted,
And when reminded of the prior night's duped romp
He smiled to burn up fact, concealed his own dread.

183

HAUNTING HIM,
THE HIGH COURT OF OPINION STILL IN HIS HOLE

So he must die who screwed him who was since split.
Still sex-reversed self-death saw girl where was man:
He missed male wholeness once to let his code-im-
Bued own self-concept bind own whole-sensed limit!

The marred blight of his world owed stain of himself!
His John must die then live sexed ruin in whose mind
Drink would erase in time . . . He waxed on such plan,
On his own power remembrance to self-bring death!

He tried to drop the jeers down of the mob's jeers,
And tried to stem the visuals that obtruded
To cause him see his period-blood's source.

Opinion's tribune loomed before him whose blood
Slid from his girl hole for his mind's court put worse,
The shrinking public right midst of his viewed butt!

184

HOW HE BIDS A PERFECT CRIME'S MATERIALIZATION

The same night suited him to leave no sign shown,
To leave his John humped in his girlish-willed turn;
His plan in time could re-surprise their dwelt norm
And let him do his will then leave the crime's town.

He parted once the trick so-earned for time blown
His keep to melt one's in his deed owed male form;
He slept in his own room; then to use spilled morn
He bettered rope moves well to use on next moon.

Willed not to re-embrace his scorned friend/traitor,
Francesco practiced on the dummy worked up
Out of his room-own bed-sheets that he tied there.

He garroted the dummy till skill bored hope.
Sun climbing he packed rope and knife to feel dare
Him fondle cloth-in tools on street till burned rough!

185

A WEEK BROUGHT TO A CLOSE MIDDLE OF WEEK

Time brought earth Wednesday second in relit date.
Once more remembrance of a past possessed them,
Although no more did pleased mood vie to set them
In eased means using friendship to find taste-sweet.

But in pretend both could be friends their hates hid.
Sure he would sail without fail Tuesday he steamed
To be stuck in Trieste! Ah I should walk he said then . . .
But fact saw need for *murder* which June eighth bid.

Again revolved to middling day week's stored time,
It was in step to fact Francesco stepped out
Without good-morning said to Johann poor then . . .

He followed on pure instinct though soon felt doubt
His friend could be found. If to sigh he turned round
And went to their hotel some time to write brought!

186

ANTICIPATION

The trick soon entered their hotel when stepped up
And went to his John's room who rose to greet him.
The two walked up and down the room one stating
How on this eve for Wednesday one would ship off!

The lading was complete was word from his mouth.
Now joyful for the thought of Rome's new meeting,
He spoke of things to tempt him wished outsetting:
Acquaintance he invited to reside loved,

And told him of the palace of the cardinal,
And promised should he come to *show* this to him,
And prove how in high place he went revered well.

On some impression's over-stimulus went
The trick to step back to his room which there still
Impelled him who returned to his friend owed end . . .

187

THE THIRD DARE:
FRANCESCO DARES GIOVANNI TO SHOW HIS MEDALS OTHERS

The great romantic the bloke was brought pretense
To bear on point return when handkerchief claimed
To leave in his John's chamber though not this seen
His friend produced one better there to trade hands . . .

It being closer than arm's length which made sense
To use between them this his handkerchief seemed
To draw them in a stumble which both's live length
Brought into heart-space linen touched in cadence!

More Johann wiped a tear from heart he held cried,
And held paused handkerchief on breast of this trick,
The young man all-loved hence all-treasured this said.

How then behave except inquire would guests each
At meal be shown his medals so that if great
Were seen to them were seen beside himself's like?

188

SAINT PETER
AT THE WILL OF A KEEN BLOKE INCURS A FIGHT

Denied twice when, twice let, denied the third time,
A strange heir of Saint Peter seemed the man then!
Strength said I do not wish to draw attention!
Francesco: Why not be willing to tell of you their kind?

Johann: I do not wish to be known here in person!
He sat down finding reason in his tensed mind:
Such wish should be respected none to grant mean.
The conversation done he sat down more bent.

On this his trick drew impetus to throw on
His neck the noose the garrote which he tightened!
A deep volcano blew in force updrew him!

So Johann showing force of nature willed then
His neck his own like few beasts evils brought them,
And got his footing to fight off this trick-fiend.

189

HOW ALL UNSUSPECTED A TRICK IS FOUGHT OFF

Surprised how soft him showed his power drawn on,
How should Arcangeli much know one soft's power?
The fight revoked the rope's use so now rolled there
The two in hot grips, hot breaths, hot in thrown spin.

As praise of softness, one soft fought the young lion
With power owed the story long wished love's mirror.
One soft was for the story pledged from whole care,
To move it forth to some end told of bound triumph!

Much less than poise would be the ruin of how much
Devotion which marched centuries brought down till
The soul was found to change the world of cold souls . . .

So not to ruin the chance of world fame's found self,
Soft Johann fought dumb ego's narrow-most cause,
Although he found poised with a knife so dumb will!

190

HOW SLIPS THE KNIFER'S EFFECT OUT OF HAND

Willed slashing rendered both men disbelief's child!
See how one learns he is the beast shown slaughter?
See how one learns he shares the butcher's matter?
If it could end soon both might learn from each well.

The fear of thing less finished drives such thief's will.
So right up to the end one willed to be sure
Must push the motive which were better left there,
An egg or sperm to grow up knowledge helped still.

The lion no man but thief will claim no town more;
The victim will not lie in strangled peace bound
To strike some other hour who swings the room's door.

A blood is shot from veins to touch the reached one,
Who has no time to change from clothes less honor,
Who has to run doomed till the first of beasts down!

191

APPALLING HAZARD
OF THE WINCKELMANN EFFECT BOUND TO EXTEND IT

The thief of life runs wild when sure the slashed man
Will die from panicked knife use though his problem
Is more than one man's knowledge of his soul's pain,
Is townsmen's knowledge of it more than matching!

He botched the murder thus self-pain told each man,
Told each man he was sex-reversed when drowsing,
Told each man he was plumbed on rectum's rousing,
And turned a girl though being a man too-rich thing!

The incognito Johann must own his fault,
How he botched his tremendous fame with this love,
As though cheap sex should blow devout of self-rule.

He needs to own up to the love most wish off,
And not in triumph's pair-sublime twin selves whole
Stand marriage of his fame with riff-raff reached up!

192

A STAG IF IT BLEED

A servant moth to light went to the heard noise,
And saw top-lie on victim whose stressed face turned
Toward the door he entered tripped with great scorn,
As raced up that to thrust him down for door's use.

So one thrust down stood up to raise on shared cause
The guest though found he raised himself in bled form,
And bid him let his speed to bring help be run
Like ran off without coat or hat one murderous!

On for a week stained ran though soldiers stride-walked,
Upending brush, inspecting sheds, entering homes!
The wounded lurcher met a maid whose fright took

To run her out of sight her part thus quite nonce.
Still then to seek, still seen to bleed, still quite shocked,
He neared the stairs to tend help use ere die once.

193

LEFT ALIVE TO CONTEND WITH IT

Said of Johann: The dread fact of own victimhood should crush him,
But fate this swift should cause incensed of protest!
He must contend the fate through various methods,
The first rise up for sign of what was done him.

Appealing to the guests who might read such man,
He groped to the great staircase now stood noticed:
O look on what he did to me screamed his voice,
And he looked showing disbelief who showed them!

Different Guests: Signor Giovanni! Signor Giovanni!
He nodded feeling double disbelief then.
Obtain him . . . .! He has murdered just the man me!

His life went through his mind in pictures slipped in.
He held hope town would capture the unreined he
Who did this to him, pooled blood to view death in!

194

ALL OF THEM TO HESITATE WAIT ON IMPETUS

Soon crowd-collected near the staircase numbers,
As *numbers* seemed own red drops on blue carpet.
He thought he must impress on else unsure dread,
A thousand years the moment for unstrong hearts

To hesitate thus look to him shock-numbed peers:
Who was to move first seemed the question for it!
A reason both on pause found while he there bled,
To wait none start his topple on high-found stairs!

Out of their rooms to find that he could tend drop,
Would numbers burst steps of a man to rise bounced?
One soon would break from their inertia lent stop.

At length one bold was found to loosen his noose:
As just the noose it seemed was holding him up,
He now fell though was carried quite to his rooms!

195

UP WITH A MERCIFUL LITTLE HELP

The guests themselves walked who bled up to his room
And lowered him in bed to lie between looks.
The fact of incident was plain in seen strokes:
A hand was pushed down on the bleeding chest wound,

A hand was pushed down on the bleeding hip's wound,
And towels were brought that with some entering tucks
Saw bloody hands replaced, both bloody hand-stalks
Wiped off in front of who in towels still bled on.

The skin that ever wrapped him keeping blood in
Was punctured so how wish more to be modest?
The whole mess was due out with men's close noting!

The hurried first steps waited on more process-
Succinct code which a doctor wished brought to them.
In clothes with towels put his looks looked a puppet's!

196

IN WEIGH OF FRAIL LIFE

A doctor on the Osteria Grande's roster
Appeared in time to solve his *question* said weighed.
To come should leave one stationed to his rest-bed—
His death-bed soon pronounced the somber doctor!

An officer the court sustained soon stood near,
To gain his information beating reached death . . .
The victim help-undressed, the doctor dress-wrapped
The vivid wounds to slow the flow of blood more.

The victim wondered could the wounds be stitched up?
The cuts went too deep, priest not surgeon wanting.
Well he must write his will said Johann raised up.

Some paper found was brought him with his own pen,
He seen to dip in ink pen when will trailed off . . . ,
As though crowd-shied to form his will there room-in.

197

HIS INCOGNITO SLIPS
AS JESUS-LIKE HE FORGIVES HIS ATTACKER

A clerk stepped past who bound Signor Giovanni—
Own pause watched in his pen-held self-relation—
And owned that he was trained to take dictation.
As breath so-wounded took caused pain in spent sigh . . . ,

More mindful to take breaths no deeper than he
Would use in sweet pain he ditched pause when said then
A great man who shaped Thoughts on Imitation
Of Greek Works lies in blood, this one the man I.

One word was heard in jinx for three grown humbler:
The clerk, the doctor, the officer in chorus
Said Winckelmann, their sounds ones in ring somber.

Yes I am he . . . Said now was one's I thought him
A man of such nil count . . . Still that man's flourish
A great man took down . . . I forgive him such crime.

198

MEDALS

The officer who did the court's work sighed plain:
Herr Winckelmann I do trust this thing told us,
But does some proof exist so I could hold thus
You to be he the self-identified man?

To mention it the travel box was breached then:
The medals which crowned heads bestowed on who rose
Were raised in view of the eccentric who chose
As documents for proof of birth gold's bright same!

Herr Winckelmann indeed was voiced in that room—
A birth room but the opposite of that too.
His first thoughts on the motive cause of that done . . . ?

Johann: Who knows but if he least must wish great fate too—
In dream to slip into the role one great won,
If least could cause who earned this enter shadow . . .

199

THE INIMITABLE POWER OF FERVENT EARNEST

The officer was sent the Osteria Grande
Who outranked one who first told court the odd news;
The clerk who outranked one who first did took notes;
The surgeon showed up ready who outranked the

Old doctor first seen . . . Such high-titled men saw
The same scene cause them to despair if show touched;
The same pronouncements would occur from those mouths
High dignitaries used to tend the same be.

The priest the final personage to show up,
He could dispense with more respect than earned his
Trust to hear told soon-sought of sins men voice up.

But Johann though could welcome God could furnish
No sins just went blank . . . Sodomitical of love
The cue of priest went . . . ! Sinless said one's earnest.

200

EVEN IN DEATH A BORED MOMENT
IS HIS TO CAUSE A FINAL REFLECTION ON HIS SUMPUOUS FINAL PORTRAIT

Still it was sorriness itself that someone
Would do this to him who was caused to pool blood!
He Johann was to die, so knowing but the sole good,
When great life went to loss on will of one dumb!

Still he was vain enough in one slumped moment
To wish a mirror brought him which how much told!
Yet he deemed he looked not worse than when too bold
He sat hours for the recent portrait shown him . . .

He soon remembered words to cross his mind then,
Who seeing his face said *such* man should be tossed on
The corpse-cart when it passed, so ready seeming!

The portrait shamed him with regret whose views on
The general scheme that art required his pinch-thin
Nose, hollow sockets, sunken-low cheeks drew down.

201

THE BOUNDLESS ZONE

The high-ranked councilor willed up in that brought
His set to ask him who hoped he leaned spared more:
More questions sure to fail use seemed too arts-poor,
His heart soon to put breath in words if great loved!

The high-ranked commissar willed up the met group
To put in staged pursuit of the slipped murderer.
The sacrament stood met in use of order
And the extreme rite stood said for his head's droop.

Time's world stood Wednesday in rotation-due spin,
To let earth spin to Wednesday this week on though
To leave twelve noon quite till it four hours drew on!

Here then on time he died on clock-four bounds new.
Who his self mattered no more to soul *new*-dawned,
If though teemed mortals lived piqued on the one so.

202

A WILL,
A DEATH ACCOUNT, AND A TRIBUTE BOOK

His will swam witness-drawn to show he spoke that
His things including book rights should end left him
The Cardinal Albani whose house dwelt him
And dwelt his things till the Albanis sold it.

The court commission's death description told that
He died through Christian courage, hence forgiving
His murderer his heart come through sweet feeling
To wish him near to offer hand one so let

To sense from this sign how love reconciled two.
One who showed great in his department one's chief
Supplier wished bonding—be no danger lie in self too

Who *murdered* him—inspiring to the deep brow
Who wrote up The Last Week of Winckelmann's Life
And left for men such record read of meek few.

203

DOCUMENTS
AND THE THRALL OF MORTALS PUT TO USE THEM

The thing that one possesses no means shown sound
To help him leave should be thought for one bears up.
Yet sooner men observed this when this world solved
And caused peers to possess some documents bound . . .

The *questioner* who life-observes men's doom-owned
Bonds that pose ones else documents should tear up!
The DOCUMENTS word said produces theirs stopped
And each of times produces theirs owed some shown.

So should who tears up his own question men's place,
And question native country though born that's bound,
And question each held motive found in leaned space.

One born free was Francesco son from wealth's zone,
Although no heir than caused to live crime's banished
So documents could not produce when breath found!

204

A PLEASURE COOK
BEING AT THE PLEASURE OF PRINCE OR COUNT

One born inside Campiglio near Pistoia so Tuscan,
His sire owned property in neighborhoods pieced.
His son sixteen trained side-long under who pleased
A Florentine prince through meal-skilled vocation.

Year second this was done sole turned first cook in
The house of one Count Bardi who—because guest
Once earlier of house of that prince brought feast—
Was brought with introduction one of cooks hung!

His need to heighten pleasure of the count's meals
Who so spoiled could feign bored disinterest in food
Was the mind puzzle of the hung one bound wise!

His doing blessed for five years' time the lent count,
Then pleased in house of one Count Baldinotti's
Till told to escort his son down sought Wien's road.

205

A COOK TO FIND THE LOW HOLE IS THE MOUTH

The peasants who broke backs in fields would do so
To time's end dulled from punishment their toil was.
A better thing was to be near some's spoiled cause,
In house dwelt prince or count his leisure could owe.

How to concoct some pleasure to make count glow
Was let to cause the riddle one hung's choice posed.
The spoiled took meals on point of form to owe use,
Although willed up to feed for space of mouths two.

Such idle men caused hours-long toil for meal plans
Of no end need to taste things swept down on cook.
So he shed meal plans for impromptu dalliance . . . !

Tired of the excess, tired of the discards so chucked,
And tired of so much mess the product each time's,
He pined for else than feeding to ones spoiled muck.

206

A SON OF BALDINOTTI'S NOT IN HIS SIRE'S MOLD,
AND HIMSELF THIEF OF COTTALDI'S GOLD-PIECES

The escort of count's to-learn son served five weeks!
Despite how wished for son his sire's pose-same use,
The son seemed not the girl his father seemed most,
As their bound stops told he was come to feel sexed!

On dismount top to feel turned his wish-tried cheeks,
He saw the bottom his sire should spawn lent cause
And earned a hard slap in the face still then pushed
Down in the sheets till cries brought others live each!

He went from this to offer cook-meal service
To Count Cottaldi though this man found so spoiled
That he found his incumbent role gold-dared thief's,

To redistribute wealth to his poor-shown self.
Shown rich would need to keep nice freedom or else
Another bottom soon would need if though slapped!

207

A HUNGARIAN LADY

He carried some six hundred of gold-pieces
Near Pressburg hoping he could enter through Wien
To Italy disguised in a Hungarian
Dress posing in the fairer of the sexes.

He showed with this some proof of beauteous traits,
To mean he could be prettified if caring,
And in concealed deception run on errand
So strength exist to haul gold in such stitched dress.

Still chance would fate that easier was reached Wien:
He was sent there in expedited travel
Once stopped in bid of the police who searched him.

The gold the thief saw swiped to owe men's evil:
Wien's Criminal Court sentenced him to served time
Of four years then to banishment from that vale!

208

A NICE LITTLE HOME

The marriage of the Archduke Leopold caused
A pardon for some part deemed served of sentence
On souls including thieves who times lived in chains.
He got out thus on tool owed one else brought use!

In 1767 she got out thus,
A girl who stood there looking just the springtime's.
The two took the same road in banishment's sense,
And love was pardoned in the marriage both chose.

Once he betook himself to Venice he brought
Her with him with the money which she brought him,
This being four hundred thirty-six coins' rich gold.

He put with this gold seventy of money owed him,
Enough to furnish the small place dwelt these loved,
Up till their money dwindled when one pushed on.

209

MULLING ON TEMPTATION'S USE

In August 1767 he went
The first time to Trieste for situation.
Two weeks spent in the heat of that month's causing,
He on return remembered things thought self-meant.

On more thought he could feel himself one destined,
To use the Osteria Grande for the place men
Were seen in transit trade itself thus tracing,
In times these should be drawn if come to meet him.

The men in this port owed to trade were there found
Without their wives though sure were even hornier
To owe being free of family most men served bound!

The love illicit he saw with the sworn-pure,
The great Almighty who endowed one's pure-shown,
And his freed up his most could men's stream corner!

210

WEALTH'S SELF ON THE RUN

On sole thought he returned to town Trieste chanced
To use the Almighty's tool to woo time-chanced him,
The connoisseur of great things be though one's limb
The great thing shown in excess of ones meek men's!

His own that limb should serve for model each tend's,
His form showed willed or not in drawn consumption,
To lend impression his limb bound world-drawn men
To point to such with members in place each dreams.

His was men's wished condition just whose loved self
Would compensate them for the missed endowment
The great Almighty brought just him in shown wealth . . .

He now skipped town of those men who pursued him,
He running for his life when those of shrunk pelf
Were joined on mouth's use but to cook the cook him.

211

CAUGHT

One free beneath the stars how was this man found?
An earth sealed up tends no browsed man's supplier,
And need must cause him fix men's structure higher,
And one traced for his portion's need ends run down.

One comes to need provisions on each scene bound,
And world's tight structure one's willed-up identifier
Supposes this which holds one to the fire,
And does like did then when caused trip the run one.

Men's brusque-said word of DOCUMENTS to be said,
He was discovered without his which tipped off
The chief that something here peculiar was met . . . !

Caught in Planina, sent to Adelsburg, he stepped up
To prefect of the Circle owning his crime *most* dread,
Was ordered under escort to Trieste, then swept off!

212

THE MAN
WINCKELMANN WAS WHAT TO FRANCESCO ARCANGELI?

Men's growing interviews grew stress for life's thief,
And ran lengths of hard questions on his forced self.
One time went forced one's how move in the circle
The great man drew to his renowned high-lived self . . . ?

He was a client, I was a pick-up he helped.
Opposed nosed in with structure's use of world's will,
To drive the questioned to divulge in words till . . .–
He did not seem too great or high the thief quipped!

He was a passing John was said but this was too high
He thought not thrilled to give name-proper status
To someone murdered . . . : He was just some old guy!

Did he know of his wealth . . . ? I doubt he had much.
I could have swiped his medals . . . More is how I,
I bled a period male period for that puss.

213

THE MAN
ARCANGELI WAS WHAT TO THE POWER OF STATE?

Men's lust pounced on the interviews-met poor self
Now to submit if not for one's mount then group's!
Once told how he could end he grew in mind hopes
To enter cabins with those ruled the world's milled.

So under force of questions their sweep forth willed
He would emit speech it of bosh in streamed throbs:
His John went killed because one of disdained Jews,
Or one of spies, traitors, or some other word spilled . . .

One over his head out of his mind slough-slopped
Down through interrogation's slough-formed record,
Till under the most strict mount his time moved up.

Once up to them to round him with thing-stiff heart,
He could explode his mimed part forcing up sobbed
Bosh on the sense that he was screwed in this world.

214

THE ABSOLUTE
BOUNDS OF IMMOBILIZATION SET ON THE ONE TO SUFFER ARREST

The dread the misdoer feels when starts the feeling
To scourge the soul of him intrusion's world wracks
Is no proof of pronouncements of men's pure reach,
Minds backing order through the loop of high wing!

The trembling dread of misdoer owes less guilt than
His sudden stumbling on the powerful shared takes
The social puts in right mime for world theirs stacks,
One octopus opinion's multiplied reign.

The fact of nature helps the man whose soul forms
In that time-deep world to know no death matters
But one's own when on look dies each life so burns!

The fact of culture trips him up through said words,
Ones prepossessed mouths use like ever used terms
To sweep up one unstopped will on the fate cursed.

215

THE ABSOLUTE
EMPTINESS OF THE MOTIVE OF PUBLIC SERVICE

The world's set structure seems so unreal when one
Is born one boundless in time's else-conserved code
That this finds some to swing or pitch for their truth
And strike or thrust to self-fix nets force sends long.

How else does the unreal *become* real thence stung
The souls who find the will to fix their world's mode
So none survive the truth of such their served truth,
Who die of self-destruction bound for being wrong!

So was Francesco Arcangeli's dire strait,
Who could not fix in mind the force that swept him
Up in time's else-conserved code his mind-poor bait,

Until it did so he perceived the real then.
The world's set structure fixed him in his cursed fate,
Did without backing but of void when stripped him!

216

THE ABSOLUTE
MONARCH ULTIMATE POWER OF THE AUSTRIAN HAPSBURGS' EMPIRE

Wrought power Maria Theresa Hapsburg Empire's
Own Empress who well functioned to bestow gold
On the esteemed son of the Empire's brought rule
Would hear of mercy for no self drew crime's curse.

The wheel existed for such bearers of time's worst . . .–
To stop the shudder she could feel touched noble,
With shudder she could not feel for the crime-bearer troubled–
A shudder stopped with one to spare the line hers.

The wheel existed for convention-forced reach,
The thing done since the mime was there to serve it . . .–
The routine rote that brought unquestioned service.

One sordid stabber punctured skin that there bled
One noble for no reason, reason's world stretched
So the unpunctured bled when bones to pierce did.

217

THE ABSOLUTE
EMPTINESS OF THE MOTIVE OF PUBLIC JUSTICE

In times men's breeches went no lower than their knees,
In times short of their long-swept modern trousers
The State showed bristled through men's set of tortures.
The modern mode required to turn from poor rites

Was some time off but things produced for world's wills
Were bound to keep connected spoils in mirrored force:
Silk, wigs, horse power truth-join things to serve worse
The rack, the wheel, the irons shown men's *burst* selves.

So was the social movement Jesus' great death
And scourged Saints' held opposed to nerve-real punish-
Ments never one embraced for justice-staged State?

The man still whole was ordered to be broken,
And this world's things the products that bring oneness
Supported with connection the deed tokened.

218

STARK BELOW THE BLUE:
ON A SUMMER'S DAY THE INFAMY OF STATE POWER OCCURS UNSTOPPED

The hung blue of the dome shone hung with question.
Still is entombed in shine the feel this timed deed's,
A tone owed place neared with remoteness when this
And dark-stood void behind the blue seem present.

More execution seemed brought through entêtement
To tend bound the event seen owed the thing wretch;
More blueness-housed indifference sent its fine reach
Out over earth's brushed space touched each horizon.

On such sweep's backdrop thing no matter what was
To find life's blessing to occur should those loomed
So will though without backing than showed blue dust!

The point the blue or point the sun took stood grown
With will the crowd brought to observe in close views
A breaking long in hollow echo of one.

219

STARK BELOW THE BLUE:
A MAN UNDER THE BRUTALITY OF A STATE EXECUTIONER

The man who brought men pleasure was to hang first,
And then break with a wheel to wield in sweeps down,
And then this wheel support limbs bent to wrap round
The outer rim to look a hex-sign strange-harsh.

This happened much like said, Francesco hanged first
And then cut that on gallows wood he slapped down,
A squirming though immobile lump of breaths drawn
In suffer-long rasps past a pinched throat's rent parts.

His slumped state seemed one perfect to receive well
The thrown drops of a wheel held so to break bones,—
And hear the squish of blood to sound while lived still!

So rendered soft on bone-breaks felt to make wounds,
He watched one wrap his limbs to line the great wheel
A grim fat executioner's in stage rounds.

220

YOU BILLIONS,
THE THING THE HANGED MAN DISCOVERED DIED WITH HIM

Sure this man found how vain men's fix on manhood,
The totem of those used for strength's consumption!
How vain most moments to devote to doomed them,
How vain the lust, pose, pride, whoop of each minute . . .

Sure this man let the vain mime bait him when stood
His mind-in totem with his length went through men,
To domineer more subtle-posed length-owned them
Although retain for girls proud unplumbed manhood.

Would men were not so hurt to hear weak girls' rants;
The weak show strength to call self-questioned strength weak;
It hurts to hear ones weak show strength in wordings.

Too men so love girls' praise that their hearts' strengths seek
To be the idol powerful in pure clench,
A big dog each through raised-up ego's ranged sake!

221

YOU BILLIONS,
THE WORD'S POWER OF WINCKELMANN SURVIVED THAT DID

The child he was owed sweet enchantment's magic
And world of then ranged cosmic through its fairies.
It takes real fairies to make prettier eras
And not his times could grow the fairies' tastes sick.

The traitors to themselves would ditch things basic
Or nature when found in earth's world untarnished!
A general scheme to owe stood nature's world was
A basis-true foundation how not tragic

To end removed from fairies should will theirs pure.
Own little friends were teaching tools he read well.
In noble simplicity in calm grandeur were

The Greeks like parents who held true in selves real.
Own fight grew evident to this child searched more
His wept poor whose hearts saw his high ideal help!

222

WINCKELMMAN
IN THE POSTHUMOUS BUST-LENGTH PORTRAIT BY ANTON MENGS

Mengs saw his friend's now-final portrait when heart
It grew in him to wish redeemed time-thinned looks!
The final truth of love-caused murder dimmed much
The portrait's lustre though its brush oils went world-

Deep to unveil cause in the weakened strength's sort
He showed midst copious enrobement's fine strokes.
The skeleton in rich undress left Mengs touched
And vowed to right this with oils took his friend forth

In portrait record done from first remembrance
Of Johann when his flesh-fat full-cheeked roommate
Was new in Rome to make his high-souled entrance!

Now in one modest bust-length portrait one's death-
Touched tone found oppositeness for redeemed sense—
So tempted less those placed fault in such man's self.

223

STILL IN LOVE
WITH THE IDEAL MALE FORM NOBLE YOUNG MEN EMBODY

The model man beloved male took back town Rome.
Berg's Paris life spent Rome life spent went married,
And on his spread estate in Riga reared bred
Each up to five sweet children in home-town owned.

Such was a thing that Johann wished for ones shone,
Who should perpetuate fine form in children tarried.
But little more this Friedrich R. von Berg did,
Well lived his life in commonness like shown bound!

He Johann sometimes wrote him from the great world,
One he still plied with works of pen . . . Friend I loved
You more than any living thing on this earth.

The line like ones sent Lamprecht, Stauder, he loved
A form the best males took who said of his heart
Not time nor age nor chance can change it—this love!

224

HOW WINCKELMANN
SUCCEEDED TO INSPIRE THE MODEL OF A MONUMENTAL TOMB HIS BEAUTIFUL OWN

The ideal male form model men took deemed health
And truth one's heart loved were he sensitive-souled,
The substitutes were what for men more stiff-souled
If not bonds grown to tiers which ordered men's real,

The vertical world's structure drawn from signs male,
And idol worship with the sex part left out!
The child more grown the friend of man in this whole
Own form of love-strong friendship entered himself,

The self to know till burst the bonds men stacked up!
One sensible to maleness loomed to hold high–
In secret worship what code-fixed world's each group–

How wished wake sleeping men to their own beauty!
He did though died more male on male to reach love,
The winged male tells in mourning so is brought sigh . . .

ACKNOWLEDGEMENTS

The writer wishes to acknowledge the help he received from ones else to be in his position to write then publish this book though acknowledges them in silence to owe how it is well to elude the records of men; those who did help know themselves to be the ones he means to note for deserved praise; but to consider how connected each is if is in the world even the full list eludes him; let each's own feeling of having helped in greater or smaller part be the thanks he wishes he could share . . .

ABOUT THE ORIGIN

The poems collected out of numbers else to comprise the book Zenith in the Will of Love, being written in Tri-cities Washington state from 2022 to 2024, were shared in various sets with different groups of people some of whose enthusiasm encouraged Scott Worth to publish.

ABOUT THE POET

Autistic, queer, culture-loving but dissent-owning, human-faced contender but animal-rights campaigner, Scott Worth is a warehouse worker in Washington state who feels grateful to people near him for finding merit in his poems, this slim volume of 224 his first-ever-published book.